Woodcutter Werebear

(Saw Bears, Book 2)

T. S. JOYCE

Woodcutter Werebear

ISBN-13: 978-1537786704
ISBN-10: 1537786709
Copyright © 2015, T. S. Joyce
First electronic publication: March 2015

T. S. Joyce
www.tsjoyce.com

NOTE FROM THE AUTHOR:
This book is a work of fiction. The names, characters, places, and incidents are products of the writer's imagination or have been used fictitiously and are not to be construed as real. Any resemblance to persons, living or dead, actual events, locale or organizations is entirely coincidental. The author does not have any control over and does not assume any responsibility for third-party websites or their content.

Published in the United States of America

First digital publication: March 2015
First print publication: September 2016

Editing: Corinne DeMaagd

ONE

Kellen Brown stared at the flower arrangements in the cooler in the produce section of the grocery store. He'd been standing here for five minutes, trying to figure out which bouquet Brooke would like best. A grin took his face. She was coming home, and everything was going to be okay again. The Ashe crew had been broken without her, but now she would be back, and they would all take good care of her so she'd never have to leave again.

His uncle used to bring his mother roses. Mom always said they were her favorite. With a frown to ward off the memories, he picked a bouquet of pink roses, then rolled the wonky-wheeled cart toward a bored-looking cashier.

"Looks like you're having a party," the woman in front of him said so softly. Even with his oversensitive hearing, he almost missed it. She was a mousey-looking woman who'd managed to hide herself completely in an oversize, red-and-black flannel shirt with clunky boots over black leggings. Her dark hair was down and long, covering most of her face.

A flash of stunning green froze him in place as she glanced at him, then away.

"Yeah," he murmured. "Brooke is coming back home. Such an occasion deserves a celebration."

The woman swiped her credit card for the small amount of groceries she was purchasing and gave him a confused look. "Well, this Brooke sounds like a lucky woman."

"She is. We all are."

The woman couldn't hold his stare—not even for a moment. He drew air into his nostrils, scenting her to see if his suspicions were true.

Fruit body wash, the soft smell that girls possess, and an undercurrent of animal struck him. "I know what you are."

"What?" the woman whispered. She gave him another flash of those stunning eyes she was trying to keep hidden, but this time, they looked scared.

"I don't know which exact animal you are, but I know *what* you are," he clarified.

"Thank you," she said to the baffled-looking cashier who handed her a receipt. With a frown for Kellen, she practically ran out of the store, her plastic bags of food bumping her legs.

Kellen sighed as he watched her leave. He'd never been good with women, or with anyone, really. He made people uncomfortable for some reason. Tagan, his alpha, said people just didn't understand him or the way he was raised, but sometimes it felt like more than that. Sometimes it felt like he'd never be able to hold a conversation with anyone outside of the Ashe crew.

That revelation made him lonely.

There was an old Coke machine outside the store—one that sold glass bottles of soda. He always got one when he came into town, but when he saw the woman waiting on a bench out front, he bought two.

Kellen settled the cart against the backrest so it wouldn't roll away, then sat down beside her. "I'm sorry I made you mad. Forgive me?" He handed her the cold bottle and popped the top of his own.

She took the bottle slowly, leaning away from him as if he was handing her the working parts of a bomb. "There's nothing to forgive. I don't know you."

Damn, she was good at hiding her face. He wanted to see her eyes again, but she'd pulled all that dark hair in front of her and wouldn't tilt her head his way.

"You shouldn't sit by me. My boyfriend will be here any minute to pick me up, and he'll be very angry if he sees you talking to me."

"Why?" Kellen asked.

"Why what?"

"Why would he be mad at you talking to another person?"

"Because that's the way men are. They're jealous and possessive."

"No. That's not the way they have to be. It's only the way some men *choose* to be. Here, let me." Kellen opened her soda, then handed her the metal top.

"You said you know what I am," she whispered.

8

"How did you know?"

He smiled at a mother bustling her trio of young children across the street. "Because we're not so different." Without any thought, he reached out and ran the knuckle of his finger from underneath her chin to the base of her throat.

The woman froze but allowed it. "You shouldn't do that. My boyfriend…" She couldn't seem to find any more words.

"I'm Kellen Cade Brown," he said. When she didn't answer, he asked, "What's your name?"

Her attention darted this way and that, everywhere but at him. "I shouldn't—Skyler. My name is Skyler."

"Beautiful name for a beautiful woman," he said matter-of-factly. With a nod of his head, he tinked his bottle of soda against hers.

"Your girlfriend wouldn't like you saying those things to another woman," Skyler said.

"My girlfriend?"

"Brooke. The one you bought the flowers for."

"Oh, she wouldn't mind. She's nice."

"You're strange," Skyler muttered.

Those two words gutted him. Sure, they were

true, but he hadn't wanted to hear that from her. He wanted Skyler to see him differently than everyone else did. He hunched inward against the pain. "Yeah." He choked on the word as he stood. He smiled at her but she wouldn't see it. She was still doing a bang-up job of avoiding his eyes.

"It was nice to meet you, Skyler."

Another flash of green as she canted her head, a sharp gesture that would've told him what she was, even if his nose wasn't working today. She lowered her gaze to the toes of his work boots, and he wondered if all of her kind were so submissive.

"I shouldn't have said that," she murmured. "It was mean. I'm strange, too."

"No," he said as he pulled a pink rose from the bouquet that rested in the cart and set it on the bench beside her. "You're perfect." Kellen gripped the cart handle and avoided the urge to look back at her again for the chance to see those stunning eyes once more. Pushing the cart toward the crosswalk, he gritted his teeth against the hurt in his chest.

"Kellen?" Skyler asked.

When he turned, she was standing by the bench with her face angled toward the ground holding the flower and the full bottle of Coke in front of her thighs. "I don't think my boyfriend is coming for me. Can you give me a ride to my house?"

Kellen looked around the parking lot, astounded that her asshole boyfriend would leave her here without a ride. "Sure. My truck is over there." He dragged the cart back to her, picked up her grocery bags from beside the bench, loaded them with his, and jerked his head toward his ride. "Come on."

She followed a few paces behind, and the first tendrils of suspicion curled around his heart. He couldn't tell if she was naturally submissive or if she was scared, but the idea of the latter ignited something ugly in his gut. He didn't like when women were scared.

"Are you afraid of me?" he asked when he was settled behind the wheel and she was sitting as far across the bench seat of his truck as possible.

"No, but I should be."

"No, you shouldn't. I'd never hurt you. What are you afraid of?"

"Being seen with you." Her answer was simple and honest, but it didn't do anything to stifle the flame in his stomach.

"Where do you live?"

"Take a right on West Bridge Ave and take it all the way through town. Roger owns a cabin outside of the city limits. Roger is my boyfriend," she explained.

The way she kept saying *boyfriend* bothered him. Not because he was jealous, but because the word lacked emotion. She could've been saying *acquaintance* for as much feeling as she put in the title.

"Is Roger your mate?" he asked, testing her.

She jerked her gaze to his, then away. "You shouldn't talk like that," she warned him in a low voice.

"Is he?"

"Yes." Her voice cracked, as if she hadn't used it in a while, and the flame in his gut became brighter.

"You aren't submissive naturally, are you?"

Skyler turned the knob on the radio volume until it blared a country song at an uncomfortable level.

Fine. She didn't want to talk, and her life wasn't his business, anyhow. That's what Tagan would tell him, and Tagan knew about people. He was good at talking to them and making them feel comfortable. He was good at negotiations with the log buyers when the Ashe crew had acquired enough clean lumber to sell to the sawmill in Saratoga. If Tagan was sitting in the truck with him right now, he'd tell Kellen to drop the woman off and hightail it back to Asheland Mobile Park where home was.

A fifteen minute drive with blaring music and Skyler's occasional direction brought him to a stop in front of a large log cabin off a dirt road.

Skyler let off a shaky breath after she scanned the front yard. "Good, he's not here. Thank you for the ride." Skyler turned and graced him with a tremulous smile. "And for the flower and the Coke, too."

She was beautiful. Pert nose and high cheekbones. Thin lips in a pretty shade of pink, and those eyes. They looked even brighter surrounded by all that purple bruising.

She pushed the door open, but Kellen leaned over her lap and pulled it closed so hard the truck rocked.

"Who. The fuck. Did that to your face?"

Skyler froze, looking terrified, but he didn't give a shit if his bear was making his face look savage right now. He wanted to kill whoever dared to lift a hand to this woman—to any woman.

"He didn't mean to—"

"Bullshit. He did, and you know it. How many times?"

"Kellen—"

"How many times?" he asked, his voice tapering to a snarl on the last word.

"Holy crap," she said, cowering against the window. "What are you?"

"Skyler, I swear to everything that is wrong in this world, if you don't tell me who did this to you, I'm not going to be able to control my shift. Who?"

"Roger."

"Your boyfriend?"

"Not my boyfriend," she admitted. "My new mate."

"Did you pick him?"

"Kellen, I don't think—"

"Tell me how it works for your kind!" He gripped the wheel until his knuckles popped and raged white.

She stared at his hands with wide eyes. "Females don't pick. Males do."

"That's all I needed to know. Buckle up."

"What? No, I have to go inside before he comes home."

Kellen shot her a warning look.

"Look, he didn't hit me! I popped off, and he pushed me. I turned to escape him and tripped on the damned mat under the sink. I fell against the corner of the countertop. This was the first time he ever got really physical with—"

"It won't be the last."

"You don't even know him!"

He huffed a humorless laugh. If this woman understood how well he knew Roger, without even meeting him, she'd stop talking and come with him. Kellen had been raised by a sonofabitch just like her mate, and he'd be hanged by the neck before he saw her end up like his mom did. "I know him well enough. Buckle up, or I'll do it for you."

"Kellen—"

With a snarl, he reached over her lap and jerked the seatbelt into place. When she was fastened in, he peeled out of the yard, shooting gravel behind them, and blasted back down the dirt road. "You plan on leaving him?"

"It's not that simple."

"It is."

"No, it's not. We obviously don't have the same

traditions that you and your people do."

"Yeah? It's customary to shove on women in your crew, is it?"

"Sometimes it's just the way it has to be." Her voice rang with hopelessness.

"Horseshit. There's no excuse, no reason. You're coming home with me."

"Why?" Her voice catapulted up an octave.

"Because," he said, daring a glance at her, "I'm going to show you how a woman should be treated."

She turned her face slowly to the front window. "I'm being kidnapped."

Kellen snorted. "No, Beautiful. You're being rehabilitated."

TWO

Skyler was going to have a full-blown panic attack right in the cab of Kellen's truck.

She didn't even know why she'd struck up a conversation with him in the line at the grocery store. She'd watched him agonize over which bouquet of flowers to pick, and something about his thoughtfulness had struck her as sweet. She'd known Roger for three months, but it was abundantly clear he'd never buy her flowers unless it was to throw at her gravestone. He hated her almost as much as she hated him. He had told her he'd asked the council to be mated to her because he cared for her, but he didn't. He just wanted a trophy he could dominate so all the other warriors could see how macho and powerful he was. Roger was a grade-A, class-ten asshole behind his charming, serpent smile.

She was the unlucky one who'd been chosen by the great Roger Crestfall. He'd broken her in a few short months, but hey, he was a legacy with a bright future. She was supposed to be grateful for the life he'd forced her into.

And apparently, she was on a streak of questionable luck because Kellen had decided to kidnap her on the day Roger had demanded she be a better mate and make him dinner. One he *can actually eat this time.* Roger's words. Kellen had said it wouldn't be the last time her mate pushed her, and he was right. Everything in her had rattled with the truth of her situation when Kellen had spouted off that it would happen again.

It would, and next time it would be worse. The only thing she could do was be perfect, do everything Roger demanded, and try to minimize the risk. She had no choice if she wanted the protection of her people. Leaving him wasn't easy like Kellen had said. Leaving her mate meant banishment.

Did she love Roger? No. She was scared of him—enough to evoke some kind of sick loyalty to him so he wouldn't hurt her again.

She used to be stronger than this.

"Kellen, please take me home. I don't want to go wherever you are taking me. I want to go back where I live with my mate." Perhaps if she said it enough times, Kellen would listen. He talked in an odd manner, much too open about what they were. Geez, he'd practically outed her shifter status in front of the cashier in the grocery store. He had a blatantly honest way of speaking that made her nervous. Men didn't give away anything for free—especially not feelings.

He didn't answer, only turned up the radio like she'd done earlier.

She spoke louder. "What will Brooke say when you bring me to your place? She'll be angry."

"You speak of anger a lot, yet you aren't an angry person. You aren't mad that your face is bruised up because that prick made a bad decision. Brooke won't be angry. She's been hurt, too."

Okay. So did he collect broken women? She didn't understand. "Does your kind take multiple mates?"

Kellen threw her a disgusted look, then dragged his gaze back to the road. "We mate for life."

"Well, so do we."

"We also pick our mates. Do you love Roger?"

She wanted to say yes. Dammit, it was right on the tip of her tongue, that bitter, burning lie. If she said yes, Kellen might take her back. He thought he was saving her by stealing her away, but she'd only have hell to pay when Roger found her. And Roger wouldn't stop with her. He'd bleed Kellen for taking his trophy.

The drive stretched on and on. Every time she twisted in her seat to plead with Kellen to take her back, his face turned severe and determined and he gripped the steering wheel harder. He drove them through miles of piney forest and winding roads without a word.

She didn't know Kellen. He could be an ax murderer, and now she was in his truck, headed into the wilderness. No one knew who she was with or where she was going. She'd been so dumb to ask him for a ride. And now her stupid instincts seemed to be broken completely because she wasn't freaking out half as much as she should've been. That was a bad sign, right? When a man was charismatic enough to steal her away and she hadn't even tried to jump out of the truck once in the last hour.

"Where do you live?" she asked.

Kellen turned down the music and smiled. "You mean where do *we* live? I'm going to keep you safe, remember?"

She cast her shocked gaze out the window to the blurred greens and muddy browns that passed by as Kellen hit the gas on a straightaway. "If my mate found out I was living with you—"

"He's not your mate, Beautiful. Best you stop calling him that."

"Do you think..." Skyler inhaled deeply and organized her thoughts, then tried again. "Do you think you're my mate?"

"No! Because again, you didn't choose me. I'm not taking you away from that prick so you can be some sort of sex slave for me, Skyler. I'm taking you so you can get a break from your life and see there is more out there than some asshole with a temper problem. You gotta job?"

"Not anymore."

"Let me guess. He doesn't want you to work because he claims he wants to take care of you."

Bingo. Fuck, this strange-talking, sexy stranger was hitting the nail on the head at every turn. She narrowed her eyes at him. "How do you know so much about the psyche of a man like Roger?"

"You don't want to know."

"Yes, I do."

Kellen looked over at her once, twice, confusion pooling in the deep chocolate brown of his eyes. He cleared his throat, as if the thought of speaking about himself made him uncomfortable. "Roger doesn't want you to work because he wants to keep you dependent. He cut off your money. The best remedy for that is to take your independence back."

"I don't even know what job I would do."

"What did you do before Roger?"

"Don't laugh, but I was a skydiving instructor."

"Why would I laugh? That's awesome."

She waited for him to take it back or tell her he really thought it was stupid that she'd take such a risk at her job, like Roger had done, but Kellen didn't.

Instead, he asked, "So, did you jump out of planes with your students?"

"Sometimes I did, and sometimes I instructed them before they went up with other teachers. I was part of a team. I loved—" Her voice caught suddenly, and she swallowed her heartbreak down. "I loved flying," she said on a breath.

His startled eyes landed on her, then he directed his attention back to the road. "Did you have sex with him?"

The question was so inappropriate and unexpected, she gasped. "Kellen, you shouldn't ask things like that."

"We're friends now, Skyler. I'm going to be your friend, and friends can talk about this stuff. Did you have sex?"

A flash of red anger blasted through her, and she clenched the strap of her purse to keep from verbally reaming him. "Not that it's any of your business, but no. I've been putting him off. I told him I didn't want to until the ceremony. That's why... Fuck."

"That's why he pushed you?"

She didn't answer. Couldn't. Shame heated her cheeks as she remembered how hard he'd tried to get her to sleep with him before she'd screamed at him. That's what got her the black eye. She had dared to tell him no, and she'd gone farther and yelled at him as she denied him. Men like Roger didn't take rejection well.

"No ceremony. No sex. No mark. No mate. You're a free woman, Skyler. You can pick whoever you want. You can sleep with whoever you want. You can work wherever you want."

"Kellen," she whispered, heart in her throat. "You make it sound so simple, but it isn't for me."

"Tell me the consequences of not being with that man. Make me understand."

"I'll be banished from my people. They won't offer me protection, and I'll be alone. It's dangerous for people like me. We survive best in pairs and groups."

"Why is it dangerous?"

"Humans finding out what I am, for one. And two, my people are at war. They always have been, I guess. If I don't have the protection of my people, I'll be picked off by our enemies. They'll spit on my carcass and never think twice about my death."

"That won't happen." Kellen's hands had a strangle hold on the steering wheel. "It won't because I won't let anyone hurt you."

"You don't know how powerful my people are, and my bloodline is important to them." She sighed and shrugged her shoulders as if to ward away her misery. "Roger is a good fighter, and he was born a shifter, not Turned. He's a legacy. He's helped to win important battles, and that's how he won the right to take me as a mate. I'm a breeder."

"A breeder."

"Yeah, it's when—"

"I know what a fucking breeder is, Skyler. I'm just not buying that you actually believe that is all you are. Your people don't deserve you."

God, he didn't understand at all. It was so easy for him to judge her, but he didn't really know. This was how she'd been raised. She'd been born into a culture of people at odds with their own kind. Rules were in place to ensure the survival of her species. Apparently Kellen's people, whatever and whoever they were, didn't care about longevity.

"You want a baby with Roger?" he asked, his voice hard as steel. "You think he'd make a good father to your offspring?"

"No," she said, voice trembling.

"How long do you think you're going to be able

to put him off? What was your plan? He'll force the issue sooner or later, and you'll be hurt. And any kid you have—" A long, low snarl came from him. Kellen slammed down on the brakes and doubled over.

The truck was still rolling slowly forward, foot by foot, but Kellen had his eyes closed and couldn't see where to steer. And now, they were headed for the edge of the road that dropped off to a steep embankment. With a squeak of terror, Skyler slammed her hand against his knee until the brake hit the floorboard, then threw the gearshift into park.

"Kellen, not here."

"I can't—fuck." His breath was ragged and red crept up his neck, up a scar that stretched across his face that she hadn't noticed before. His shoulders heaved, and the air became heavy with something powerful, just above her senses.

Desperate not to die in the truck with whatever was tearing its way slowly out of Kellen right now, she reached over him and shoved his door open. Unbuckling him, she prayed he wouldn't eat her. She'd never met another type of shifter before. She was in control of her thoughts when she Turned, but would he be?

She pushed him hard, and he hit the gravel road with a thud. Curled on his side, he grunted in pain.

The keys were dangling from the steering column, and her kidnapper was utterly helpless as he tried not to shift. She could leave. She could shut the door and drive back the way they came and go back to Roger before he noticed she was gone.

Skyler gripped the door handle, prepared to shut it and speed back to her life. Back to her crappy, hopeless, fear-riddled life.

"Trust me," Kellen said in a ragged whisper.

She must've misheard him. "What?"

"Don't leave. Just trust me. Ahh!" His neck snapped backward, and his eyes watered with anguish. The soft brown color had been replaced by an intense silver, and the thick muscles in his neck strained.

Hell. Kellen was going through hell trying not to shift.

She could go back to her horrid life, or she could take a chance with Kellen. She could stay and take a break from the suck. She slid from the truck and cradled his head. "One day, and you'll take me back."

"One day, and you'll beg me not to."

She drew up short. He seemed so confident. If he knew the people he was pissing off, he wouldn't be so keen on keeping her near. "One day."

His eyes never left hers as he nodded once.

"Let him out," she whispered against his ear. "I won't leave you—not yet. Let your animal out and stop the pain."

An agonized groan left his lips and tapered into a growl. "Get in the truck."

He didn't have to ask her twice. She scampered in, shut the door, then hit the automatic lock for good measure. And when she looked up, the back of a giant beast rose above the window line.

"Son of a biscuit," she murmured in awe as she took in the full, furred, fanged expanse of Kellen Cade Brown.

He was a bear. And not one of those plump, tame ones she had seen bumbling around in a circus once. He was one ton of toned, muscled, ferocious, scar-faced, pitch-black, snarling grizzly.

As he stood on his hind legs and shook his enormous block head, she gasped at his full height. He had to be twelve feet tall. Her heart pounded, threatening to eject from her chest cavity, and a scream lodged in her throat, making it impossible to breathe.

He could rip through this truck like it was a can of tuna if he wanted to.

He lowered himself to all fours, never taking his eyes from hers, and slowly, his animal retracted until he was human and utterly naked on his knees by the truck. So, bear shifters could go back and forth between their animal and human sides almost immediately. She couldn't do that. She had to stay an animal for half an hour, at least.

His clothes lay in tatters on the ground around him. She searched frantically in the back seat for an extra set, but all she found was a folded pair of jeans on the floorboard. They smelled clean but had dark stains and tattered holes in the knees. Work pants.

She slipped from the truck when Kellen pumped his hands as if they ached. He stared down at his sharp nails, which were still retracting.

"Are you okay?" she asked, dropping to her knees in front of him. She held the jeans clutched to her chest.

"Hurts," was all he said in a hoarse voice.

Looking around to make sure no one was

barreling down the road to see this, she slid her hand across Kellen's back. His muscles were tensed, but as she massaged the knots, he relaxed little by little.

"You're a bear shifter," she said low. Tracing faint, curved scars across his back, she said, "You fight grizzlies. No wonder you don't fear my people."

Kellen huffed a laugh, then leaned back on his heels, apparently unconcerned with his lack of clothing.

His eyes were brown again, the same color as his hair, which was short on the sides and longer on top. Tousled in that sexy I-just-got-out-of-bed-and-don't-care look. It was the first time she'd really taken time to study him. She'd been working so hard to hide her face and those damned telling bruises, proof of her weakness, that she hadn't really seen him. Smile lines bracketed full lips with a scar on one side, and his eyebrows were dark and animated. His neck was thick with muscle that led to perfectly defined pecs and tiny pert nipples that had drawn up against the stiff breeze. Bulging muscles flexed across his stomach with each ragged breath he drew. His shoulders were broad and defined, and his chest rippled as he dragged a hand through his chestnut colored hair, as if his scalp still tingled from the Change. Strips of muscle hooked over his hip bones and delved toward his thick, long, half-mast erection. Embarrassed at staring, she jerked her gaze from between his thighs and looked at his face again.

His eyes dropped to her outstretched hand, and she gasped and yanked it back. When had she started reaching out for him?

The corners of his eyes tightened as he dragged his gaze back to hers. "I don't mind if you look at me, Skyler."

She shouldn't. She was promised to Roger, but crouching here, in the middle of nowhere, it was so tempting to do something she wanted to do instead of something she was told to do.

With her gaze, she traced his ribs, pressing against his skin with every breath. His strong arms and his long, lean legs folded under him. With a steadying breath, she allowed herself to look at his thick, hard erection standing rigid between his thighs. She released her breath slowly, then handed him his jeans.

"Thank you," she said, shrugging off the embarrassment that blanketed her.

Kellen didn't look uncomfortable at all. In fact, he seemed to be studying her reaction. "You touched me. My back. You rubbed my back. Does that mean you aren't afraid of me anymore?"

"Why does it bother you so much whether I'm afraid or not?"

"Because I'd never hurt you. I'd never let anyone hurt you. I don't want you to be afraid. Not ever. Why did you just thank me?"

Her cheeks were on fire, and she dropped her chin so her hair covered her face. "For letting me look at you and not making me feel bad about it. Roger isn't my type…" She squeezed her eyes tightly closed at her misstep. "I mean—"

"No, say what you want to say." Kellen lifted her chin and smoothed her hair away from her face, then brushed the lightest touch over her bruised cheek. "I like it best if people just say what they mean. I get confused by games."

"Okay." She believed him. He spoke differently, more honestly, so she could see how it would be confusing for someone like him if she only offered half-truths. "I don't like the way Roger treats me. His meanness has made me dislike everything about him.

The way his hair gets greasy when he doesn't wash it and the way he smells like cigarettes and onions. The way he looks at me, like I'm the dirt he stomps off his boots and onto the floors. You have been nice to me. You gave me a flower and a soda, and you look at me like I'm somebody special. And I..." She closed her eyes so she could find her bravery. "I like the way you look. If any of this had been my choice, I would've picked someone who acts and looks like you."

"So, I'm your type?"

Opening her eyes, she looked at him as sadness washed through her. "Yes, but it doesn't matter."

Nodding slowly, he conceded, "Maybe not."

Unfolding the jeans, he stood and slipped them on, then looked at her with a slight frown.

"What?" she asked.

He pressed his hand to her lower back and guided her around the truck, then helped her in. Reaching over her lap to fasten the buckle, he looked up and said, "If I was built for a mate, I would've picked someone like you, too."

THREE

The dilapidated sign above the hood of the truck read Asheland Mobile Park. Kellen's truck was one of those white, monster-looking trucks with fat tires and a lift kit that didn't have the best suspension anymore. Skyler lurched back and forth as he seemed to hit every pothole in this ratty trailer park.

The yards were mowed, and there wasn't a single plastic pink flamingo in sight, but she'd heard horror stories about people living in these little communes so far out in the woods. Probably making moonshine. Or even worse—maybe this was some kind of meth lab community.

"What do you do for a living?" she asked suspiciously.

"I'm a lumberjack. So are the rest of the Ashe crew. We've got two crews clearing the dead, beetle-infested wood from this area, us and the Gray Backs. The Boarlanders do the cutting for us before we start on a new job site."

"Lumberjacks?" She hid a grin. "So, you must like pancakes then."

"What?"

The relief at him not being a criminal—an illegal substance criminal, at least—had her giggling like a lunatic. "Never mind. It's a Paul Bunyan joke."

A slow smile took his lips as he pulled in front of a trailer that read 1010 on the door frame. "I like the way you laugh."

"I laugh like a hyena," she muttered.

"I think it's cute."

Skyler frowned and stared at him, waiting for the punchline, but he didn't offer one. Instead, he hopped out of the truck. She did the same and studied the trailer he was headed for. The tiny home was painted a light cream color with dark green shutters and a rusty red door. It was small, a singlewide, and ancient.

"It looks drafty," she observed, fidgeting.

"It is. And it has a resident mouse you'll do best to ignore. We keep taking him out, but he just comes right back in. He's a part of this place. Denison named him Nards, on account of his giant—"

"Testicles," she finished. "How charming. So Denison lives here?"

"No, Ten-ten is yours. Brooke used to live here, but when she gets back from the city, she'll be moving in over there." Kellen pointed to a trailer across the dirt road from where they stood.

A pang of something unsavory slashed through her. She'd forgotten about Brooke, but now guilt bombarded her. She shouldn't have looked at Kellen naked. He was taken, and Skyler wasn't interested in stepping on another woman's territory. She got what he was saying. When Brooke returned from wherever it was she'd been visiting, she'd be moving in with Kellen. An image flashed across her imagination of Brooke and Kellen making love tonight. The walls of 1010 looked paper thin, and no doubt she'd be able to hear them. A nauseous, unexplainable feeling punched her gut as she followed Kellen inside. Why shouldn't he want to have sex with his mate? She'd been away from him, and he had every right to enjoy himself with his woman. It shouldn't make any difference to Skyler.

But it did.

She resented Brooke for catching such a good man. Sure, he was a too-honest-for-his-own-good kidnapper, but he probably treated Brooke like a queen. How had Skyler been so unlucky to garner the attention of master-manipulator Roger, who'd probably never said a kind word to a woman in all of his life? And now she'd been stolen away by this sexy-as-hell woodcutter werebear who was utterly unavailable. The unfairness of it all stacked up like brick walls around her heavy heart.

Kellen should've just left her back at Roger's house. She'd accepted her life, and now, it wasn't good enough anymore. Tomorrow, she'd go back to Roger, and it would hurt ten times worse to absorb the awful things he said to her and the insulting names he called her. She'd resent him even more for what he'd done to ruin her life. Her crappy fate would've been easier to bear if she'd been allowed to continue to guard her heart and not wish for more.

The turmoil swimming inside of her now was all Kellen's fault.

"You want the tour?" he asked.

"No. I think I can find my way around a singlewide trailer home without your help." Her voice snapped like a rubber band, and she hated how it sounded. She was polite and non-confrontational by nature, but this was all too much. Roger was probably losing his shit by now wondering where she was, and by the time she went back tomorrow, he'd be furious. A black eye was going to be the least of her worries.

Kellen frowned at her, but nodded slowly, then strode toward the door. "Oh," he said, turning. "We're having a little celebration tonight for Brooke's return. I'd be honored if you came. With me. As my…" He ran his hands roughly through his dark hair and sighed, then tried again. "I'd like it if you let me sit by you." His nostrils flared as he inhaled slowly. "I mean, I want to feed you and take care of you."

Okay, he'd been doing a good job of asking her to the party until the last part. Who said stuff like that? He wanted to feed her? Was it a fetish perhaps? But he was staring at her so openly awaiting her answer, and as strange as his combination of words were, they pulled at something deep within her. Something she'd long thought was dead. He wanted to take care of her. Even though he was paired with Brooke, he was still friend enough to want to show her how a man should treat a woman. "Okay."

A slow smile crept across his face, and he approached her slow. "Yeah?"

"It's not like I have that much of a choice, Kellen Cade Brown. You kidnapped me, remember?"

The smile faded from his face, and he crooked a finger under her chin until she lifted her gaze to his. "You can escape this place anytime you want. Your will is free here, Beautiful. Go with me because you want to. Not because I'm making you."

She nodded once, and his eyes dipped to her lips. The humor she'd seen in his expression a second ago didn't exist anymore. The air grew heavy around them, like it had in the truck, but this time, it wasn't uncomfortable. It was warm like a blanket and settled her nerves. He touched her cheek, then cupped the back of her neck gently with his oversize hand. His thumb stroked circles into her hair, and with his other hand, he tucked a dark tress behind her ear, away from her face.

She was exposed here in front of this almost stranger, but for the first time in a long time, she felt like someone actually saw her. *Her.* Not what she could do for him, or how important her bloodline and children would be. Kellen was looking at her as if he knew her down to her bones.

Slowly, he lowered his lips to hers. She should run. This was wrong. They were promised and bound to others, but he held her in his gaze, and she was transfixed and helpless to flee. Angling his head, he pressed his lips against hers. She was surprised at how soft they were. He was scarred—a tall, wide, hard man who filled the air around him with dominance. His lips should've been demanding, but they weren't. They plucked at hers with tiny, sexy smacking sounds until she leaned into him and stood on her tiptoes for more. Wrapping her arms around his neck, she opened her mouth to allow him to taste her. His tongue brushed hers in the softest touch, and a delicious rumble filled his throat. She'd done that, pulled that sexy noise from him. She nibbled on his bottom lip, and he gasped. His expression went completely blank, and he moved away as if to escape her, but then he leaned in again and held her tightly against his chest. Stroking her hair, he said, "I shouldn't have done that. You aren't ready, and you need to be alone to find yourself before a man touches you like that again. I'm sorry."

Done what? Kissed her? Hell yeah, he shouldn't have done that. He had a mate, and he was currently soaking the panties of another woman—namely her. But he was rocking slowly back and forth, crushing her to his sternum, and the guilt just kept piling up and up. He wasn't worried about Brooke. He was worried he'd kissed Skyler while she was still traumatized by Roger's abuse. This was all so confusing.

A lump formed in her throat, suffocating her as he squeezed even harder. Panic froze her as the repercussions of what she'd just done with him set in.

He hadn't just kissed her.

He'd changed her.

"I think you should go," she whispered.

Because she was definitely about to fall apart, and she didn't want him to see her shatter into a million pieces of broken, messy Skyler. She was porcelain right now. Raw, fragile, and spider-webbed with cracks so thin they were almost invisible. But all it took was one more blow, and she'd be nothing but sharp edges and dust.

"You want me to leave?" he asked, sounding hurt.

"I need you to."

His throat moved against her cheek as he swallowed hard. "I'm sorry," he said again, then turned without another word and left her alone.

It was hard to keep her sobbing quiet. She knew what he was now, and it wasn't a lesser shifter. He wasn't a field mouse or an otter. He was an apex predator, born to sense everything in his territory. He'd hear her hitched breathing and quiet weeping, but she didn't want to share this heartache with him or anyone else.

She wasn't his problem. Her insecurities were her own.

She padded through the tiny living area and kitchen to the bedroom where a neatly made queen-size bed took up the middle of the room. Bracketed by two windows covered with pretty blue blackout curtains, the room was darker than the rest of the house. This was it. Her sanctuary. This was where her heart would break. And for the first time in months, it felt okay somehow. She hadn't dared to shed a single tear in the cabin she'd lived in with Roger. He'd hate her even more for feeling anything at all. But here, for reasons she couldn't understand, she felt safe to let her demons out.

Quietly though.

She curled up under the soft comforter, pulled a pillow close, and held it against her face as she screamed her fury at the world. At the people she'd been born to and Roger's unfortunate attention. For what he'd done to her. The bruises on her face and the scars that Kellen wouldn't see, because she'd never let him witness what Roger had really done to her.

When her throat had gone hoarse and felt lined with glass, her cries of anger turned to weeping for what Kellen had shown her. He'd given a broken girl a flower and a soda, just because he was a nice person, but he would never realize what he'd really done.

He'd made her want.

He'd made her need more from a pairing than a demanding mate who would hurt her in the bedroom someday. Who would strip her down to nothing but bone and marrow until she didn't feel anything.

Kellen had made her life unacceptable with a kind gesture. He'd kidnapped her, sure. But he'd done it because he honestly thought he was saving her. How could she resent him for that? Her own father hadn't come to her rescue when she phoned him and explained the horrible things Roger called her. Roger had grabbed her arm so hard it had bruised fingerprints around the inside of her elbow for days. Dad hadn't come. He'd told her to *buck up. A mating wasn't supposed to be easy.*

But Kellen made her think that a mating shouldn't be this damned hard.

That's when her crying turned pitiful.

Kellen. She was drawn to him, had been since she watched him pick out flowers in the grocery store, but he'd never be hers. Not even close. He hadn't taken her because he liked her, he'd kidnapped her because he pitied her, which was the worst part of all. She'd done a fantastic job of hiding her predicament from everyone, bar her father. She'd managed to live in her own private hell, wishing something would happen to free her from the mess she'd found herself in, and when her sexy, bear-shifter knight in shining flannel swooped in there, it had been scary, liberating, and empowering.

But he belonged to another.

God, she was pathetic. Pining for some strange-talking man she didn't understand who was in love with another. He was a stranger. This had to be her heart's desperate attempt at latching on to the first man to show her kindness.

Her tears ran dry, and she hiccupped and gasped until she couldn't cry anymore. Her head ached, her eyes were swollen, and she probably looked like a psychotic raccoon thanks to her unfortunate decision to wear mascara this morning. But deep inside, she felt a little better. What was it about crying her eyes out that released all of that ache she'd been harboring? She should've felt like a weakling, but instead, she felt more clear-minded than she had in months.

Roger wasn't it for her.

Her life had meaning.

All it had taken was a few hours with a nice stranger to show her she had more value than a fertile womb and the bloodline that ran her veins. She inhaled deeply and hugged her pillow to her chest.

But...the banishment.

Her epiphany didn't matter. She was utterly and unfailingly stuck in this lonely life.

Nards, the mouse, crept across the dark wood-laminate flooring, dragging his giant testicles behind him, and she couldn't help a tiny smile. She wasn't alone after all. Her gaze arced after him as he sped up and disappeared under the bathroom door. Her gaze met a pair of silvery blue eyes, simmering with emotion.

She gasped and sat up.

Kellen was crouched on the floor, weight shifted on one leg like he'd wanted to escape but couldn't.

"Kellen! How long have you been there?"

He hunched his shoulders at the shrill pitch of her voice, but dammit, that sob-fest had been meant for a pathetic party of one.

"You were crying," he said.

"I know. I wanted to do it alone."

He dipped his chin and canted his head, eyes on the bed skirt beneath her. "No one should cry like that alone."

"Yes, they should, if they *want* to be alone."

He frowned, looking entirely baffled. "Oh." He shifted his attention to the door where several tall, sexy-looking, sweat-and-dirt-streaked men hovered. "She's okay."

"You sure?" A stocky man with a shaved head and a tattoo down his neck asked. "She doesn't look like she's okay to me."

"Who the fuck did that to your face?" A Nordic-looking man with slanted eyes and shoulder-length blond hair asked. He appeared savage in the dim light as shadows stretched across his furious face.

"Drew," Kellen warned.

"No. Explain, Kellen. You brought a woman up here, and she's all banged up and crying. We need to know what's going on."

"She ain't just a woman. Not like Brooke was," Kellen said, standing slowly. "She's a shifter. Been beat up by her own kind."

"That true?" Drew asked.

"The man I'm promised to"—she circled her finger in front of her face—"did this."

"Why?" a sandy brown-haired man with a beard asked.

Kellen handed her a box of tissues, and she wiped her face and tried to smile. It hurt. "I wasn't being a good enough mate."

"Fuck that," Drew said in a careless tone. "Who is he? We'll fix him up right for ya."

"No!" she rushed out. Lowering her voice to a more tolerable level, she repeated, "No. Kellen was nice enough to take me away to give me a little break from him, but I don't want this starting some shifter war or anything. It's fine. I'm…figuring everything out." She licked her dry lips and said, "I'm Skyler."

Kellen handed her a Dixie cup of cool water and said, "Skyler, meet the Ashe crew. We all work the mountain to the east of the trailer park together. That's Drew." He pointed to the Nordic-looking man. "Haydan is over there," he said, and the man with the tattoo and shaved head nodded once in greeting. "Denison is the ugly one with the beard, and Brighton was born to the same sow."

When he pointed to the two men with light brown hair and light facial scruff, she thought Kellen had to be teasing by calling them ugly. They were very handsome. "You're brothers?"

"By blood. The whole crew feels like family to us, though," Denison said with a kind smile. "We've been together for years. My brother over here don't talk, but he understands just fine."

"Hi, Brighton," she said with a shy, two-fingered wave.

Brighton smiled, his green eyes crinkling, and he nodded. He pointed to her face, and the smile dropped from his face. He looked sad.

"It doesn't hurt much anymore," she lied. "It happened Thursday."

"I'm Bruiser," an imposing man with muscular arms the size of tree trunks said from the doorway. "We'll get out of your hair, but if you need us to gut the man who did that to your face, just say the word. We've been itching for a fight since Connor and Jed—"

"Bruiser," Drew said in a harsh voice.

The behemoth frowned. "Right. You probably wouldn't want to hear about all that. If you need anything, just holler."

The crew of disastrously good-looking lumberjack bear shifters shuffled from the room. Brighton approached and touched her shoulder, and Denison did the same before they left. She understood. Touch was important to most shifters, and it did make her feel comforted that these strangers didn't seem to mean her any harm.

Apex predators they might be, but mindless hunters they were not.

Kellen jerked his head toward the window as his eyes took on a faraway look. "They're back."

"Who?" she asked.

A slow, stunning smile took his face. "Brooke's home."

FOUR

Dread slammed into Skyler like a punch in the gut. It was hard to draw breath as Kellen rushed to the door. "Come out when you're ready," he called. "I want you to meet her!"

The front door banged closed, and she imagined him and Brooke running toward each other and clashing into each other's arms.

But she was an adult who'd only met Kellen this afternoon, and no matter what her traitorous heart was trying to tell her, she didn't have feelings for him like that. He was an acquaintance, a friend at most— that was all.

And as his friend, she needed to support his relationship with a woman he obviously cared for deeply. With a sigh of determination, she stood and made her way into the bathroom. Nards was nowhere to be found, so she stepped up to the sink and stifled a yelp. She looked like hell on a hot day. The make-up she'd attempted to cover the bruises with this morning had run off. Her mascara streaked down her cheeks, the oversize flannel shirt she'd been hiding from the world in made her boobs look saggy, and her nose was red. With a strangled groan, she splashed water over her face until her make-up was completely gone, then shimmied out of her red flannel button-up. Underneath, she wore a red tank top with tiny black polka dots that hugged her slim figure. Roger never would've let her wear something so revealing in public. He'd said he didn't like people seeing too much of her skin, but fuck it all. She was smack dab in the middle of a trailer park overrun by badass bear shifters. If Roger had a problem with what she wore here, he could take it up with their canines.

She knelt down, feeling the stretch of her favorite pair of black leggings, and re-tied the laces on her dark hiking boots. When she stood, she was determined to make a good impression on Brooke and the rest of the people here. She liked the Ashe crew. They didn't know her from Eve, but they'd offered to go after Roger when they'd seen the bruises on her face. In those few minutes she'd conversed with them, they'd won her loyalty.

Running her fingers through the soft waves of her long, gnarled hair, she rushed to the front door. With a steadying sigh, she rallied her reserve, then threw the door open wide and hustled onto the small porch.

She'd expected Brooke to be beautiful. How could she not be to have caught the attention of a man who looked like Kellen? And she'd been right. Brooke stepped out of a silver Volvo in front of a trailer across the dirt road. It was hard to make her out through the crowd of men around her hugging her up tight. But through the shifting bodies, she could make out long, curled blond hair and animated green eyes. An easy smile and laugh lines. Kellen handed her a box of wine and the flowers, and she doubled over laughing before she side-hugged his waist.

Their interaction lacked chemistry. Skyler frowned. She'd expected to have to witness kissing and groping, but Kellen easily passed her off to Denison for a hug. A lean man with dark hair and blue eyes she didn't recognize sauntered around the back of a black pickup truck and clapped Kellen on the back. They murmured something much too low for her to hear and laughed.

Then the man did something incomprehensible. He leaned over and kissed Brooke square on the lips. It was one of those tender, romantic, all-in-with-the-feels kisses that made Skyler blush for witnessing.

Kellen jogged over to Skyler, but he stopped at the porch stairs, and his eyes went round. "You look…" He left the word unspoken as his eyes raked over the tight fit of her tank top, leggings, and her clunky boots.

"I don't understand," she said on a breath. "I thought Brooke was yours."

Kellen angled his head and narrowed his eyes. "My what?"

"Your mate?"

"Brooke?" he sputtered. "She's Tagan's mate. She's mate to the alpha. I care for her deeply. We all do. She's the only female in our crew, and she's the best of us. She's my friend, not my mate."

Skyler felt stupid and tricked. "But you bought her flowers."

"Because she deserves them. And wine because she likes it better than the beer we drink here. She's a real lady, and ladies deserve for men to do sweet things for them."

Kellen looked innocent and baffled in the waning evening light. He also looked a little upset.

"I'm sorry," she said, relief flooding her until she was lightheaded. "Every time you spoke of Brooke, I thought you were talking about her because you loved her."

"I don't have a mate." Now he sounded offended. "I don't deserve one, and it isn't my fate to protect a woman like that. All I'll have is Brooke, my friend." His shoulders drew up near his ears, as if he was embarrassed, and a soft blush touched his cheeks.

"Hey," she said, desperate to comfort him. His uneasiness was her fault for making assumptions. She jogged down the stairs and touched his hand, then looked up into his eyes, now churning silvery-blue again. "I made a mistake. I didn't know."

She squeezed his hand, and he looked down at where their palms touched with a confused frown.

"I'm glad she isn't your mate," she whispered.

His startled gaze crashed into hers. "Why?"

Uh oh. Okay, she shouldn't have admitted to her feelings like that. She wasn't in a position where she could pursue a relationship with anyone, much less with someone who felt as dangerous to her heart as Kellen.

"I don't know why I said that." She shrugged and dragged her gaze to the toes of his scuffed work boots.

"No games. Why are you glad?"

Her breath trembled as she was caught by his eyes, demanding she be honest.

His chest heaved under the T-shirt that clung to the sharp angles of his defined chest. He squeezed her hand again and whispered, "Why?"

"Because…" She wasn't good with words and couldn't think of any way to explain how strongly she felt for someone she'd just met. Instead of speaking, she pulled his hand over her racing heartbeat, just under her collar bone. "Because this."

A slow smile stretched his lips as he canted his

head and felt her pounding pulse against his hand. Slowly, he drew her hand over his breastbone and pressed it against the hard muscle there. His heart was racing hers. "Me too," he murmured.

"Kellen?" the man from the truck, Tagan, asked. "Who is she?"

Kellen swallowed hard, breaking the spell and pulling his hand away from her. "Tagan, this is Skyler."

His alpha gave him a long, hard look and blinked slow, then brought his icy blue eyes to hers. "I know what you are, and I'm pretty sure I know who your mate is too. Roger Crestfall?"

Skyler nodded but was compelled to explain. "He isn't my mate. Not yet. There's been no ceremony."

"And your face. Did he do that to you?"

Brooke stood right behind her mate, looking at her with ghosts in her eyes.

Skyler's breath hitched at having to explain something so painful to people she wanted to like her. "He pushed me. The counter helped with the coloring."

"Your people could bring trouble to mine," Tagan said low.

"Tagan," Brooke said, her delicate eyebrows drawn down. "She's been hurt."

"Which is why I need to know what you are doing here, seeking sanctuary with my Second."

"Second? Kellen, you are Second to your alpha?" Skyler hadn't realized he was so high in the crew.

Kellen's nostrils flared as he inhaled slowly. "I took her," he said, turning to Tagan. "She was hurt, and I couldn't stand taking her back to him—to Roger."

"You *took* her?" Tagan asked, his eyes narrowing to dangerous looking slits.

"Wait. He kidnapped you?" Brooke asked, turning her attention to Skyler. "Against your will?"

Lying was out of the question because shifters could hear a false note of a half-truth. Dammit. "Kind of?"

"Kind of?" Tagan roared. "Kellen, you can't take someone's mate!"

"Not Roger's mate yet," Skyler squeaked out.

"You know what Skyler's last name is?" Tagan asked, his voice too loud for comfort. "Drake. She's a fucking *Drake*, man. She's a legacy, and her father is on the council."

Kellen was shaking his head like he'd never heard of her last name before, thank God.

"I don't understand," Brooke said, gripping Tagan's arm. "What does her last name have to do with anything?"

"It means," Tagan gritted out, "Kellen has kidnapped a fucking princess."

"Wait, wait, wait," Skyler said, holding her hands out to calm the crazy names being thrown around. "I'm not royalty. I'm just from a long bloodline."

The muscles in Kellen's throat tightened as he swallowed. He angled his chin and looked at her like he'd never seen her before, like he was regretting what he'd done. It gutted her.

Tagan scrubbed his hands down his face and glared at Kellen. "She's trouble for us. You brought her here, you fix it. Take her back."

"To Roger?" Kellen asked.

"Yeah, to fucking Roger Crestfall. You don't understand the dynamics of her people, Kellen. Hell, I only know because they are in our territory, and an alpha is supposed to keep track of that stuff. Any threat to my people, I need to know about. She can't stay."

"I think we should hear what Skyler has to say about it," Brooke said in an even, unintimidated tone.

The woman was Skyler's new hero. She was having a hard time not going to her knees with the heaviness of the dominance in the air, and Brooke was standing up to her alpha. Between Tagan and Kellen staring each other down and drawing their animals to the surface, Skyler could barely breathe.

"Fine." Tagan nodded, his eyes sparking with fury. "Speak."

"I don't know what to say."

"Did Kellen bring you here against your will?"

"Yes."

"Do you want to go home to Roger?"

"No."

Tagan's lip lifted in a snarl as Kellen stepped in front of her. "Fuck!" the alpha yelled, the curse echoing off the mountain.

A low, dangerous-sounding rumble came from Kellen. "She's not going back."

"You kidnapped her!" Tagan bellowed. "That's not how things work. You don't just pick a woman and take her like some caveman."

"That's how it works for me!" Kellen yelled back.

"I don't do things like you or like Denison or Haydan, or like Jed did. This is how I do things. This is how my mind works. She was hurt, and all of me wanted to rip Roger's entrails out and hang them from the trees. That's what I wanted to do. You wouldn't approve, so I didn't do that. I stole her away from him instead. It was the best I could do for my bear. Look at her face, Tagan. Look at it! If Brooke looked like she did, would you send her back to her abuser knowing it'll get worse for her? Knowing she would get hurt again? Would you? Don't talk to me like I'm abnormal. Like I don't know how to interact with people. I didn't kill him. Ten fucking points for me because I wanted to, and I stopped the urge. I don't know a lot about talking to people, but I know what I can and can't handle. If I left her there, my bear would've returned tonight and killed Roger in his sleep to free her." His voice dipped low and helpless-sounding. "I couldn't leave her then, and I can't send her back now."

"Do you care about her?" Tagan asked, hooking his hands on his waist.

"Yes," Kellen said without hesitation.

Tagan narrowed his eyes and tilted his chin. "As more than a friend?"

Kellen nodded slightly.

"Change," Tagan demanded.

"I don't want to challenge you."

"You did when you took a Drake without consulting with me first. Change."

Kellen's shoulders lifted in a sigh, and he spun slowly toward her. He pressed his lips gently on Skyler's forehead. "Go on inside."

"What's happening? Are you going to fight him?" She covered her mouth with her hands and sucked in air. "I don't want you to fight." She ducked around Kellen's wide shoulders and pleaded with Tagan. "Please, I didn't want to come at first, but I think I'm supposed to be here now. I want to be here. I feel…fuck." Tears stung her eyes as she searched for a way to keep Tagan from hurting Kellen. "I feel better than I have in months. I'm not worth fighting over. I'll go if you'll just let him be."

"No," Kellen snarled. "You aren't going. You're safe here. I want you here with me where I can make sure no one hurts you."

Brooke looked at Kellen with the saddest eyes. "Come on, Skyler." She pulled gently on her hand.

Burning tears streaked down Skyler's cheeks.

"But I don't want him to be hurt."

Tagan lifted his chin, and something slashed across his eyes for just a moment before it was replaced by fury again. Approval perhaps.

"They won't kill each other," Brooke promised as she pulled her onto the porch and through the front door of 1010.

Kellen watched her somberly, and just before the door closed behind her, she called out, "I'm sorry!"

Her sobbing was eclipsed by the roaring of the bears.

FIVE

Brooke stood on her tiptoes and stared out the peephole in the front door. "Yep, you definitely don't want to watch this."

An inhuman bellow of pain and another of rage rattled the trailer, and Skyler wrapped her arms around her stomach as if it would keep her insides intact. She was breaking apart again, and her urge to change made her gasp in pain.

"Skyler? You look ill. Oh, shit. You can't Change in here. Trailers are the worst kind of place for that. Here, let me get you a drink of water. Why don't you sit down on the couch and take some deep breaths."

Skyler did as Brooke suggested and curled up in a little ball, determined to stay in her human skin. She didn't change if she didn't have to. Not anymore. Not after the last time she'd done it with Roger.

"Here," Brooke said, handing her a glass.

Skyler sat up and drank thirstily. The sounds of the raging bear fight were softer now. Perhaps Tagan and Kellen had dragged the battle off into the woods that surrounded the trailer park. Or maybe one of them was dying.

A wave of pain doubled her over.

"No, no, no, listen," Brooke crooned. "Kellen is fine. He'll come back a little bruised up, but he'll start healing immediately. You'll see. Tagan and Kellen grew up together. Tagan's mom found Kellen when he was a cub, took him in before a foster family could figure out what he was. My mate wouldn't ever really hurt yours, Skyler. He's a new alpha and needs to be swift with punishment if one of his bears puts his crew in danger. That's all."

"Tagan's new?" Skyler asked, set on carrying on a conversation that would distract her from the horrible imaginings of the battle going through her head right now.

"Yeah, he challenged the last alpha, Jed, a couple of months back. He…well, Jed ordered whoever turned me into a bear would win me. A shifter named Connor tried, and when Tagan moved to protect me, Jed tried to kill me."

"You're newly Turned?" The ache in her middle was easing as her curiosity took hold.

"Yeah. I didn't take it well," Brooke said, huffing a laugh. "I went back to my home in the city. I was angry at Tagan for putting a bear in me. I was angry with Connor and Jed and already dealing with my own issues from before, so it was all too much. I wanted to learn how to control my animal by myself without them coddling me. Are you a bear, too?"

Skyler clammed up because she was definitely not ready to talk about that part of her life with Brooke. Now that she knew she wasn't competition for Kellen's affection, Skyler wanted the woman to like her. She didn't know why her approval meant so much, but Kellen said Brooke was the only female around here, and it had been a long time since she'd had a girlfriend. Roger had cut off any chance she had at making friends in Saratoga, leaving her lonely. But Roger wasn't here, and what he didn't know wouldn't get her punished.

Brooke opened her mouth, as if she were about to ask what kind of animal hid inside of Skyler, but then clamped her mouth shut. Instead, she asked, "Do your people have alphas?"

"No, we have councils for each side of the war. They keep the peace between the people on each side and make wartime decisions. Then come the warriors. Then come the men who do nothing for our kind. Then the children, and below everyone come the females. The breeders. I'm no princess like Tagan said. I'm nothing at all."

"Bullshit. Your people sound like assholes."

"You said Kellen was my mate." Skyler gripped the cool glass in her hands and dropped her gaze in shame. "It felt nice to let you think that, but it's not true. He's not mine. I belong to Roger."

"You belong to yourself. No man owns you, Skyler. Take it from me, who spent a hell of a lot of time as a human. This," she said, pushing Skyler's hair away from her bruises, "is abuse."

"Not to my people. The men call it 'breaking a willful mate.'" She snorted at how dumb that seemed now. She'd been raised to accept it, but here, away from it all, it just sounded like more manipulation. "I probably seem pathetic to you."

Brooke knelt in front of her and looked her square in the eye. "No. Any man who did this to your face is pathetic. Was this the only time he was rough?"

Ashamed, Skyler shook her head. "It was the worst, though. Please don't tell Kellen. His bear already seems hard to manage."

Brooke frowned at the door. "He isn't, usually. You affect him. Usually Kellen is the level-headed one of the crew. Come on. I want to show you something."

Brooke pulled her upward until she was steady on her feet, then tugged her by the hand until they reached a second bedroom Skyler hadn't had the time to explore yet. In it was an easel with a large, messy painting of a man's face. A pile of similar pictures, built up with black and gray acrylics, sat in the corner. Brooke spread them out until they lined the floor.

Skyler didn't know much about art, but she could almost feel the pain coming off the pages. In one picture, the man was smiling, but his grin was soulless and didn't reach his hard, cold eyes. In another, the corners of his lips were turned down as he stared out with disdain. He looked terrifying.

"You said I probably thought you were pathetic," Brooke said, as soft as a breath. "This man hurt me. He broke me."

Skyler jerked her head up and stared at Brooke. "How?" She seemed so strong and sure of herself. How could anyone have hurt her?

"He attacked me in a stairwell in the city where I used to live. He hit me, bruised up my face like yours is now. Then he marked me here." She ran a fingertip down a long, healed pink gash across her neck. "He wanted me to always remember how helpless I'd been. And for a while, every time I looked in the mirror, I did feel helpless. But I wasn't, and neither are you."

"When Kellen took me, I was scared," she admitted low. "But deep down, I was glad someone was trying to save me. I've hated that I couldn't save myself."

Brooke's light brown eyebrows winged up. "This is where the winds of change turn to a fucking hurricane if you let them, Skyler. You don't belong with a man who would hurt you. And if that is how your people operate, by breaking women, sounds to me like you need to find yourself new people."

"They'll banish me if I leave Roger."

"Banishment is bad?"

"The worst. I'll be disgraced all my remaining life, which won't be long, because my enemies will kill me the second they find out I'm no longer protected by my council."

Brooke canted her head and gave her a significant look. "Not if you learn to fight back, and not if you find someone strong enough to protect you."

Skyler shook her head in ready denial. "I couldn't ask Kellen to do that. He's...he's better than all of this. He's special. I don't want to put him in danger, and if he took me in, I'd put him right in the crosshairs of my people. And he said it himself. He doesn't want a mate. He only took me because he's good, down to his bones good, and can't stand the thought of someone being hurt like that."

"Mm." Brooke grunted noncommittally. "Maybe. Have you met all the boys yet?"

"Yeah, they all showed up in my room while I was crying my eyeballs out."

Brooke laughed and nodded. "Yep, they'll do that. They get all touchy feely, too, if you're upset, so be prepared for that. They aren't trying to be inappropriate. It just settles their animals if they know for sure that you're all right."

"Well, that explains it then. My people aren't like that," Skyler explained. "Touch isn't important to them."

"Is it important to you?"

"I watch people kissing and holding hands in public, and it makes me feel funny."

"Funny how?"

"Like, I think I'd enjoy that. Growing up, I was always taught not to feel anything, so touch was a no-no."

"Are parents allowed to hug their children?"

"My mom did when I was little. She was what my father called *a willful mate*, though, so she changed as I got older. She stopped smiling and singing when she cooked. I think she wanted to feel, and I never saw my dad actually hurt her, but something was happening to make her shut down. And when I was ten, I was sent off to be raised with the other breeders. There was definitely no hugging there." She cringed at the memories of the cold room she'd shared with the other seven girls her age and the harsh way they had been raised to respect male authority.

Now that she saw everything in such a different light, perhaps banishment wasn't the worst thing that could happen to her. Perhaps living a long, empty life void of affection was worse.

That realization still didn't justify putting Kellen's life in danger.

The front door banged open so hard it slammed against the wall. She rushed into the other room in time to see Kellen catch the door on the rebound. He'd rustled up some jeans somewhere, but a dark spot was spreading across his thigh, and he limped heavily into the living room. Cuts crisscrossed his chest, but none of them were deep, and most of them were already half-healed.

"Tagan?" Brooke asked.

Kellen's voice was hoarse when he said, "He's at your place. Still riled up, though, so be easy with him."

Brooke jogged out of the trailer, leaving Skyler alone with Kellen, who was currently bleeding onto the laminate flooring.

"I don't know why I'm here," he said, frowning. "I meant to go to my trailer."

"Come on," she rasped out, fighting the thick dominance that laced the air. "I'll clean you up."

"You don't have to—"

"I want to."

Time crept away from them as he stared at her long and hard. "Okay."

She led him to the bathroom, careful not to hold his hand like she wanted to do. He was still riled up, too. The silver in his eyes told her the human part of Kellen wasn't completely in control yet. And he smelled like animal. Fur, pine, and earth mixed to make a heady scent in the air. Part of her wanted to open a window to relieve some of the pressure from her chest, but a bigger piece of her wanted to revel in the smell of him. It was alluring and unfurled something deep within her. His scent, masculine and feral, called to her.

"You smell aroused," he said in a gruff voice. He settled on the side of the bathtub, his injured leg stretched out in front of him.

"You could've kept that little gem to yourself,"

she muttered.

"Why? It's sexy, and I like it. Why shouldn't I observe and compliment."

"Oh. I didn't know it was a compliment."

"You smell good, and I bet you taste good, too."

God, she hoped he was talking about her lips or skin, but from the hungry way his eyes traveled down her thighs, he meant exactly what he said. His forward way of speaking was jarring.

"My bear always wants sex after a fight. It isn't your place to satisfy that need, though, so I can stop talking about it. You look uncomfortable."

"No." She unbuttoned the snap on his jeans and sighed. "It's all right. I like that you are blatantly honest. You're a bit of an over-sharer, but it's better than hiding your feelings all the time. Just say what you want, and if you cross a line, I'll tell you. I don't want you to change for me."

Kellen tilted his chin, and the fire in his eyes dimmed. Uncertainly, he said, "You don't want to change me?"

"No. Why would I? You're..." She smiled at the memory of his first compliment to her today. She repeated it in a soft whisper. "You're perfect."

Kellen snorted, then hissed air through his teeth as she tugged the waist of his jeans downward.

"Help me, man. I can't clean the injury from behind your pants."

"Oh." He frowned, as if he'd just remembered the growing blood puddle across his quad. Standing, he pulled the denim material away from his skin and slowly pressed his pants down, exposing the extent of the wound.

Skyler bit her lip and thanked her lucky stars she wasn't afraid of blood. Four long gashes ran across the top of his leg, and the bottom one was a bit of a gusher. Kellen rearranged his face to a stoic expression and gripped the edges of the bathtub as he sat down. "If you hand me a towel, I'll get the bleeding stopped."

She turned to a pair of faded, white cabinets above a washer and dryer against the bathroom wall and found an old, threadbare black towel. But when Kellen reached for it, she swatted his hand away and pressed it on the injury herself. "How long does it take you to heal?"

"With an injury like this, two days until it's a scar."

This rocked her back on her heels. She was a fast healer, but not like that. "Hold that there, and I'll find something to clean it."

His hand pressed against hers, strong and steady, as he held her transfixed with his gaze. "Thank you."

"It's no problem," she said, shrugging it off. "I've dealt with battle wounds before."

"No, not for that. For saying you didn't want me to change. I'm... I know I'm different. Most people outside of the Ashe crew write me off—think there is something wrong with me. Thanks for not doing that."

She thought of how hurt he'd looked in the grocery store parking lot when she'd called him strange, and shame burned her cheeks. "I'm sorry about what I said when I first met you."

"Don't. You don't have to apologize for that. Everyone thinks that. It's okay." He dipped his attention to his bare feet and seemed unable to lift his gaze.

A blush crept into his cheeks, and she brushed the color there with her fingertips. She knew how it felt to be different all her life. To not fit in. "You are good, Kellen. I like that you say what you mean and how you feel. I like that you let me in."

His hair was mussed from his fight, so she ran her fingers through until it was smooth and in place again. Kellen dropped his chin to his chest and gripped her wrist so fast, she gasped. He ran a gentle thumb across the tender skin of her arm.

"I like when you touch me," he rumbled.

"I like it, too."

She liked it more than she ever thought possible. His reaction to her was empowering. He didn't bully her or manipulate her into doing what he wanted. He made her feel beautiful and in control. He complimented her and was vocal when she did something he appreciated.

The silky skin around his shaft grew thin and hard as his erection jutted out between his legs. He was impossibly thick, and she had no idea how a man of his size would physically match her smaller body, but that didn't stop her sex from responding instantly to his arousal.

"What are you thinking?" he whispered, cupping her face.

She smiled as she thought about being as utterly

honest as he was.

"Say it," he goaded.

"My panties are wet."

The small smile fell from his face and his eyes went serious. "How wet?"

"Soaking."

She'd never wanted to be with Roger. Never even wanted to kiss him, but with Kellen, it was different. She wanted him, and even better, her body already had tuned to his needs. There was no doubt they'd be compatible in the bedroom if they could get over the mismatched size issue. Kellen was too sweet to hurt her.

Kellen's gaze fell slowly to the apex between her thighs. She was already on her knees, padded by the bathmat, and she spread them a little wider for him. "You want to feel?"

Kellen's nostrils flared, and he nodded. "I don't think I should, though. You've been hurt. You need more time."

She shook her head and let him see the honesty in her eyes. "It would be nice not to think about all of that for a little while."

A small, knowing grin crooked one corner of his

sensual lips. "I can make you forget."

When she ran her fingertip from the base of his shaft to tip, it twitched under her touch. Kellen leaned his head back, thick cords of muscle in his neck stretching. Damn, he was sexy, allowing her to see how much she affected him like this. She traced a long vein under his tight skin, and he gripped the edge of the bathtub harder. She toyed with him until the head of his cock was red and swollen, ready. A bead of creamy moisture formed from the tiny slit at the tip, and she tasted it.

Kellen's arms shook, and he released a shuddering breath. "Beautiful, you're going to kill me."

"You want me to stop?" she asked innocently, trying to hide her smile.

"No. I want you to do whatever you want to."

Well, that sounded fun. When she cupped his balls, the muscles in his legs twitched. The mounds of his abs flexed and softened with each ragged breath he drew. She leaned forward and kissed each one, starting with the top of his eight-pack and moving to the bottom two. Slowly, she pushed on his knees, gentle with his injured leg, and nestled closer to him.

Stretching up, she nibbled his bottom lip.

With a groan, he cupped the back of her head and plunged his tongue into her mouth. God, he tasted so good. She opened her lips wider for him and lost all track of time. He could've kissed her for minutes, or hours perhaps. All she knew was that she was lost and falling and happy for the first time in a long time. Kellen liked her. And not just because she was a breeder or because her last name meant something. He liked her for her, the good and the bad.

His fingers combed through her hair, as if he couldn't help touching her silken locks, and when he'd had his fill of her lips, he tasted her jawline, then her neck. And when the inferno inside of her grew too hot to bear, she pulled her tank top over her head and unsnapped the front clasp of her black, lacey bra.

Kellen eased back as she shrugged out of her clothes. He devoured every inch of her vulnerable skin with his gaze. "Beautiful," he whispered, though she couldn't tell if he was reverently murmuring the nickname he'd gifted her or if he was complimenting what he saw.

Either way, it brought a smile of relief to her face. She hadn't ever asked a man to appreciate her body like this.

Gently, he cupped her breasts, pushing them inward against each other. She surged forward, pressing her cleavage against his stony shaft. His shaky breath said he liked the feel of her against him like this, so she moved her chest down so that her full breasts stroked the length of him.

His eyes rolled back in his head as she did it again, which gave her an idea. A naughty idea. She was drunk on the way she felt with him and bolder than she'd ever been with a man before. Pulling his hands away from her breasts to free them, she edged closer until he was nestled in her cleavage, then put his palms back in place once her breasts surrounded his impossibly hard cock.

Chest heaving, he pressed her tits around him and rolled his hips. "Fff—" he said, biting back a curse.

Skyler was nearly gleeful. She bit her lip hard to hide a triumphant giggle. Kellen was relinquishing control. He moved his hips against her, totally enraptured. She was doing this, causing that expression of pure ecstasy on his face. She reached around him and pressed her fingertips on his thrusting hips just to feel the power there. In one smooth move, he reached over and took a pump of lotion from the bottle near the shower, then took himself in hand and pressed between her breasts again. This time, it was slick and made a wet sound that just about buckled her. Holy cow, could she come without him touching her?

His hips bucked faster, and his breath came ragged. He was trying to be gentle so she pushed his hands, squeezing her breasts around him more tightly, and he yelled out and bucked faster. The wet sound was constant now, and the taut buds of her sensitive nipples brushed his belly as it flexed against her.

She cupped her sex. She'd soaked her panties, and her leggings were warm with her arousal. Kellen took his eyes from her bobbing chest and his dick forcing its way through her cleavage and frowned at her hand that touched between her thighs. So fast he blurred, he scooped her up and strode into the bedroom, any hint of a limp gone. He should've been in great pain, and bleeding like a stuck pig, but when she looked over his shoulder at the fallen towel on the bathroom floor, it wasn't even soaked through.

"Had to stop," he murmured against her neck as he lay her down.

"You didn't want to finish?" She was confused. He'd seemed ready to climax.

"Oh, I want to come, but not before you do."

Her belly quivered with those muttered words against her ear. He slid down her, removed her boots and socks, then pulled her leggings and panties until they cleared her ankles. She should've felt vulnerable, laid out on top of the sheets like this, the setting sun still lighting the room enough for him to see all of her. But the look in Kellen's eyes stifled any embarrassment she could've harbored about her body.

Without a word, Kellen flipped her over until he lay back down on the mattress and she was straddling his face, holding her just above him with his powerful arms.

She started to protest, but he plunged his tongue into her sex and she melted against him. He sucked on her sensitive nub as he retracted his tongue. Her hips bucked forward. Splaying her hands against the mattress above his head, she locked her elbows and rolled her hips the next time his tongue thrust into her. She would've been more embarrassed if he didn't seem to be thoroughly enjoying himself. And when she looked behind her, he was stroking himself in rhythm to the pace he set with his mouth. Three more thrusts and the pressure was too much. She called out and froze above him, pulsing around his lapping tongue.

Holy shit. This was easily the hottest thing she'd ever done. Probably the hottest thing she'd ever do again. Kellen rolled her over and pulled a pillow toward them, then lifted her neck gently. When he was satisfied that she was nice and comfortable, he kissed her slowly from her navel to her collarbone, until the head of his cock pressed an inch inside of her.

With a moan, she spread her knees wider and cradled his hips against hers. He was slow in taking her, as if he knew his size would be too much if he wasn't careful. She dug her fingers into his back as he pressed inside of her another inch and stretched her. Tiny aftershocks still trilled through her. Kellen's arms were flexed from trying to keep the bulk of his weight off her, and she scratched her fingernails down his triceps. His hips jerked, and he plunged into her. She gasped and arched against him. He seemed to like when she had her claws out, so she dug them into his back as he bucked into her, faster and harder. She cried out with every stroke as the tingling pressure built inside her. And as she breathed his name, she fell apart, detonating around him as he gritted his teeth and shot into her. Warm jets released into her as his cock flexed and swelled, pulsing to match her own release. She raked her nails down his back, and he pursed his lips and thrust into her again and again until she lay spent and boneless under him.

He kissed her neck and moved slowly inside of her, as if he couldn't get enough of the feel of her around him. He hugged her tightly and eventually eased out, only to tuck her against him and run a light touch from the top of her shoulder blades to the iliac crests of her lower back. Over and over, he stroked and kissed her, nibbled her collar bone until she felt completely adored.

This was the moment she'd remember for all time. For the rest of her short life, she'd know this was the time that had changed her from the inside out. This moment, right here, in the arms of the man who'd altered everything, was when she chose banishment.

Because a life without love, without this, wasn't really a life at all.

SIX

Kellen crossed his arms and sipped his beer, staring at the steaks on the grill. Today had been a roller coaster, and he wasn't sure how he felt. Enraptured by Skyler, absolutely, but this wasn't a simple relationship. Even if she hadn't been hurt and half-broken when he found her, he was full to the gills with his own inner monsters, none of which he could ever let her see. If she knew what he really was, she'd leave and never come back. And that was a thought that was no longer tolerable. Not after he'd bedded her. Not after his bear had chosen her once and for all. He wasn't mate material, but that didn't seem to stop his inner animal from craving a partner.

And damn his instincts, he couldn't avoid the bond that was forming between them. If he cut her off now and distanced himself, he'd still always pine. It was the way he was built. Loyal to a fault, and when he felt, he *felt*. Fuck, he was in it now, and she deserved so much better.

"You trying to burn the steaks, man?" Denison asked. "Cause you know no bear here likes their meat hard as a hockey puck."

Rushing, Kellen flipped the meat as the heat below sizzled and hissed. "Sorry. I'm just…"

"In Skylerland?" Denison asked. He tinked his bottle against Kellen's beer. "Looks like you got it bad."

Kellen inhaled deeply and shook his head in shame. "What am I going to do?"

"About what? From the way you were rocking that trailer earlier, it's pretty obvious you chose her."

"Yeah, and what good does that do either of us? She's better than this place. Better than me."

Denison cocked his head and frowned. "Is this because of the time before Meredith found you?"

Kellen clacked his mouth closed and stared at

the steaming steaks. No way in hell was he talking about his past. Thinking about it was bad enough.

Denison gripped his shoulder and squeezed. "You ain't him."

Kellen snorted and shook his head as his friend sauntered off. What did Denison know? He'd grown up with a loving family. Him and Brighton both. They were made for mates. They'd seen a good example of love. Kellen wouldn't even know where to begin. He knew one thing, and one thing alone. If he allowed himself to claim a mate, any mate, he'd burn her up until she was a husk of the person she was supposed to be.

He hadn't brought Skyler here to claim her.

He'd brought her here to heal her.

Anything more would break her the rest of the way, and it wasn't something he or his bear could live with.

Haydan whistled a catcall, and Kellen turned. Brooke and Skyler were making their way down the porch stairs of 1010 a few trailers up. Skyler was wearing a pair of skin-tight, sexy-as-all-get-out jeans and a black tank top.

"Your mouth is hangin' open," Denison called

with a smirk on his face.

Kellen clacked his teeth closed and cleared his throat. Skyler had pulled her dark hair back in a ponytail, exposing her long, fair neck, and she'd covered her bruises with some paint shit women wore to enhance whatever they thought needed enhancing. He wasn't usually a fan of heavy make-up, but Skyler had dolled up her eyes with dark stuff and the green in her irises looked downright exotic. Or erotic. His cock swelled and hammered against his jeans. Her arms were toned, and she walked straighter, chin up, like the day had done wonders for her confidence. And when those gorgeous eyes fell on him—well, she just about buckled his knees.

"Mouth is hanging open again," Denison observed helpfully.

"Shut up," Kellen said. "Take the steaks off the grill. I'm gonna...yeah." He handed Denison the tongs and weaved a path through the strewn plastic lawn chairs and around the fire pit Tagan was tossing logs into.

His alpha was staring at Skyler, too, but his eyes looked troubled. Kellen had already paid for her to be here in blood, though, so like it or not, Tagan had to accept her presence for tonight.

Kellen stopped short in front of Skyler. Brooke squeezed her hand, then made her way toward the fire pit.

"You look," he said, voice cracking on the last word. He cleared his throat and stood taller. "You look healthy."

"Healthy?" Skyler asked, then giggled. "Thank you, I think."

She stood on tiptoes, sliding her hand over his shoulder, and kissed the two day scruff on his face. Her lips were soft and warm against his jaw. Surprised, he placed his hands on her hips to steady her on the way back down.

"You look handsome."

He frowned down at his black cotton T-shirt and worn, holey jeans over his scuffed work boots. He hadn't exactly dressed up for Brooke's welcome home celebration, but if this was what Skyler liked, he'd dress down more often for her.

The sleeves of his shirt were tight, and Skyler ran her hand down his arm, over the curve of his bicep, and settled it in the inner crook of his elbow. Good grief, the woman could bend his animal to her will with a touch.

"I can't see your bruises anymore," he observed. Maybe conversation would stifle his urge to lead her back into 1010, bend her over the bed, and take her from behind until she screamed his name in pleasure.

"Yeah, Brooke has some really good foundation she got when her attacker hurt her face. She let me have it. Now I won't have to hide behind my hair anymore."

His face stretched in a smile. "I like that. I like seeing your face." He brushed his finger down her cheek. "Your eyes."

Skyler leaned against his hand, her soft jaw contrasting against the rough callouses of his palm.

"You hungry?" he asked, the urge to take care of her overwhelming.

"Starving."

He leaned forward slowly and kissed her forehead. It was a long time before he could convince himself to take his lips from her smooth skin. She was an amazing woman, and she didn't cringe at his touch. His addiction to her was growing by the second. When he finally pulled away, he said, "Come on. I'll get you a plate."

When she was settled in a seat upwind of the fire, he piled her plate high with steak, fire-grilled corn on the cob, and fruit salad. Only when she was settled and her Dixie cup full did he make his own.

The murmur of the crew shootin' the shit after a long day on the job site calmed Kellen's frayed nerves. Everything was fine. When he'd told her he wasn't the mating kind, she hadn't even batted an eyelash. She still asked for intimacy, she didn't seem mad, and she wasn't pushing him for more. He could do this. He could toe the line between too much relationship with Skyler and just enough.

Jed had done it. Shit, Jed was a terrible example. His mate had left him to live in Saratoga, a couple of hours away. She wasn't built for life mated to a logger. Or for wilderness at all, really. Highfalutin smarmy witch who berated the crew at every turn. He'd been glad when she left. Unfortunately, it ripped up their alpha at the time, made him off-his-rocker-crazy, and threw the entire crew into uncertainty and chaos.

What if Skyler left because he couldn't offer her more? What if she went back to Roger in desperation for commitment Kellen wasn't able to give?

"Hey," Skyler murmured as he sat down with his food and half-empty beer bottle. "What's wrong? You look panicked."

Her hand on his forearm soothed him, and he attempted a smile. "Just thinking." Too damned much. He wasn't a smart man. Never had been, never would be. It wasn't his low self-esteem that admitted this. He had good attributes such as loyalty, a strong back, a level head under pressure, a mechanical mind, and skill with big machinery. Thinking too much like this confused him more than he usually was and stressed him the hell out.

"Did I do something wrong?"

"No." The word came out too loud, too forceful. "No," he said, softer. "I'm just scared I won't be what you need. That I won't make you better."

The smile faded from her lips. "I don't need you to fix me, silly bear. You've already done enough. You took me away when I wasn't able to get myself out of the predicament I'd found with Roger. I can take it from here. I just need you to be my friend."

"Good. Just a friend." That word pierced him, but it was what he needed, too. His head cleared, and the jumbled mess in his mind slowly faded away. "I can be that."

Her face fell, and she slid her hand off his arm. "Okay."

Skyler didn't speak to him after that. She ate in silence as the other men informed Brooke of all she'd missed while she was away. The snake in Haydan's toilet, the raccoons that stole a carton of eggs Tagan had left unattended by the grill for too long. The rope swing the boys had tied over the creek, and the makeshift skateboard ramp Bruiser had made. Drew had jumped off a roof onto it and broken the ramp into splinters. The usual shit that often led to minor injuries and more bad ideas. Brooke shook her head and called them "man plans," but she didn't try too hard to hide her amusement.

The fireflies lit up the woods that surrounded the trailer park, and Skyler watched them with wide-eyed wonder. Kellen couldn't take his eyes off her. God, she was beautiful. She was also rubbing the gooseflesh on her arms. It was June and warm enough during the daylight hours, but nights were always cool, especially in the mountains.

Kellen stood and retrieved his jacket from his trailer, then dropped it around her shoulders from behind. Skyler jumped, as if he'd startled her, but smiled her thanks. It didn't reach her eyes though, and Kellen knew he'd failed to keep his turmoil to himself. She was smart and probably saw right through him. He had to do better than this.

He opened his mouth to ask her if she wanted anything else to drink, but Denison beat him to it.

"You sure have a pretty tone to your voice, Skyler," Denison said. "You sing?"

Brighton had been plucking away at his old guitar for the better part of half an hour now, and he looked up from the fret he was fingering as Skyler seemed to mull over her answer.

She pulled her shoulders up to her ears, as if she didn't like the attention on her. "In the shower."

"Mmm," Denison said, tapping the toe of his work boot in rhythm to Brighton's plucking of the strings across the fire. He reclined in his old plastic chair. "I bet you have a folksy, bluesy, country-sounding voice. What kind of music do you like?"

Skyler dipped her gaze to her lap and hid a smile. "Folksy, bluesy, country-sounding music."

"Name your favorite band," Denison challenged her.

Tagan stretched his legs out and wrapped his arm around Brooke's shoulders, then angled his face and glared at Skyler thoughtfully while she contemplated an answer.

"Lately, I like The Drues."

Denison nodded slowly. "You know Ash and Dust?"

Skyler's dark eyebrows wrenched up. "Do *you* know Ash and Dust?"

The notes changed as Brighton picked a slower chord, and Skyler huffed a soft laugh. "Of course y'all do."

"You better not leave me hanging on the harmony," Denison said, all but daring her to step up. "The girl's part either."

"Do I really have to do this? In front of everyone?"

"We can all sing really badly with you if you'd like," Bruiser offered.

"The hell you will," Denison said, leaning his elbows on his knees. "She's got this." He swung his gaze to Skyler's over the flames and lowered his chin. "You've got this."

Kellen fidgeted. He didn't want her

uncomfortable, and he sure as hell didn't want her clamming up from being put on the spot. Really, he wanted to protect her from all the prying eyes that seemed to make her so uncomfortable, tuck her under his arm, and run off into the woods with her.

That wouldn't help Skyler open up, though. It would hurt her if he coddled her.

Kellen's heart was pounding, and his blood was roaring in his ears, loud enough that he missed the first few lyrics Denison sang in his rich tenor. Brighton strummed louder as his twin's voice sang out.

"Said she was better off beside me
But she don't see what I do
She's way too good for a rambler like me
So I told her we were through."

Denison lifted his chin and gave an encouraging smile to Skyler. Then sang the first line of the chorus.

"Broken heart…"

Skyler trailed with the same lyrics in harmony, and Kellen drew up straight at how beautiful her voice was. Like a bell with a shot of perfect vibrato at the end, quiet at first, but building.

Denison's deep voice came in again.

"Broken time

Nothing left

She took what's mine."

"He took what's mine," Skyler trailed in complimentary, haunting notes.

"Holy shit," Drew murmured, grinning at Skyler.

"Shhh," Denison said, throwing him a quick frown, then pulled his attention back to Skyler, who straightened her spine beside Kellen, and clasped her hands in her lap.

Denison caught the right notes and continued.

"I'm ash and dust

Hopin' she's made of the same

Pack my suitcase

Board that train

Damn the weather

Damn the rain

Gonna go and get my baby."

Denison leaned back with a grin and a shake of his head. "It's you now, girl. Bring it home."

Skyler inhaled deeply and lifted her voice in soft, longing notes in rhythm with Brighton's chords.

"He said I was better off without him

But he don't see what I do

He's the biggest part about me

After all that we've been through.

Broken heart…"

"Broken heart," Denison trailed, stronger.

Skyler lifted her voice.

"Broken time

Nothing left

He took what's mine

We're ash and dust

We're made the same

Pack my suitcase

Board that train

Damn the weather

Damn the rain

Gonna go and leave my baby."

They sang a new part for Denison, stronger, with more emotion, and Kellen couldn't take his eyes away from Skyler. She closed her eyes and swayed to the music as that beautiful sound came from her. And when the final chorus was almost through, she opened her eyes and smiled in the easiest expression he'd seen on her face since he'd met her. She was stunning. The roaring in his ears died to nothing as she held one last, perfect note, then leaned back and clapped along with everyone else. She laughed, strong and free, and pulled her clasped hands up to the side of her blushing cheeks, as if she was embarrassed by the applause.

Brighton stood and gave her a hug, and Denison stepped around the fire and did the same, murmuring something in her ear that made her look so proud. Kellen was enamored into silence, watching her interact with his people like she'd always been a part of them. She was magnificent. She was commanding every attention he possessed.

She was everything.

Her eyes danced to him, and her smile faded, as if she waited for his opinion, and it mattered. As if this would all be ruined if he didn't approve. Damn Roger for doing that little number to her.

Reservations out the window, he tugged her onto his lap and hugged her tight, nuzzling her neck. "I'm so damned proud of you, I could die of it," he whispered against her ear.

She giggled and slid her arms around her neck. "That was so scary," she admitted.

"You were perfect. Your voice is beautiful, Skyler. You're beautiful." He cupped her face and searched her striking eyes. His reflection met him in the green color, hopeful looking and open. He smiled just before his lips brushed hers, floored that his bear had stayed settled and quiet all night. That never happened. He didn't have any doubt in his mind it was because of her. She settled him, made him happy and calm.

He eased back after a tender kiss and hugged her waist closer as he relaxed into the chair.

The others settled into easy banter as Brighton strummed a new song.

Skyler rested her back against his chest and took the last sip of his warm beer. "You want another?"

"No," he said, stroking his fingers across her stomach. He loved that she was small compared to him. Not fragile or overly thin, but strong and the perfect height to rest his chin on the top of her head. "I have a one beer limit."

She frowned. "Why?"

"You don't want to know."

Twisting in his lap, she rested her hand on his chest and said, "I want to know everything about you."

Kellen sighed, flattered that she cared, but

terrified she'd want to draw him into a conversation he wasn't ready for. "My old man was a boozer. I've never had more than a beer at a time as a precaution."

"Oh," she whispered. "I'm sorry."

"Don't be. I hardly remember him," he lied.

Her eyebrows quirked, as if she could hear the fib. Maybe she could. He didn't know what her senses were capable of.

Tagan came to warm his hands by the fire while his mate talked to Bruiser. Skyler wiggled out of Kellen's lap and stood next to his alpha. "Can I talk to you?" she asked.

"Shoot," Tagan said in a clipped tone.

Skyler looked around, then stepped closer to him. Kellen didn't want to eavesdrop. It wasn't his way, but he was trapped behind them in the chair, too close to get up without it being obvious, and his hearing was impeccable.

"Brooke told me what happened to Conner. I'm sorry for your loss and for what you had to do, but I was wondering if his job was available."

Tagan jerked his gaze to hers, his face highlighted by the flickering orange glow of the firelight. "You want work as a lumberjack?"

"I'm not picky about the job. Kellen said I need to earn my own way so I can feel independent again, and I agree with him. When I earned my own income before Roger chose me, I felt stronger. It would make it easier to leave him if I wasn't dependent on him."

"I thought you were planning on leaving tomorrow," Tagan said low.

"Well, that's part of what I wanted to discuss with you. I know this is a risk to you and your people, me being here. If it's too much, I'll gladly leave. But if you have an opening on your crew and are fine with me here, I'd work real hard. I'm a fast learner, too, and stronger than I look."

"Stronger than you look," Tagan said, narrowing his eyes. "Because this job isn't some easy come, easy pay job. It's hard work from sun up until sundown. It's physical and dangerous, and the crew depends on each other. One weak link could get my men hurt, or worse. I can't hire a weak link, you understand?"

"I understand." Her voice was soft and defeated as she stared at her shoes.

Tagan inhaled noisily. A muscle in his jaw ticked as he clenched his teeth. "Prove you are strong, and

I'll consider a probation period."

Skyler's eyes opened wide, and she lifted her chin until she met Tagan's cool gaze. She pursed her lips in a thin line of determination. "What do I have to do?"

SEVEN

Tagan didn't answer Skyler's question. Instead, he whistled a shrill sound behind his teeth and jerked his head toward the trailer on the end of Asheford Drive. The Ashe crew grew immediately quiet and stood as one.

"Why are you doing this," Kellen asked, standing with his friends. "Why are you testing her?"

"Kellen," Tagan barked. "That's enough. If you want her, that's your choice. It's my choice who I pick for my crew. If she can't prove herself, I'll find someone else to replace Connor. Someone who has half a shot at not getting one of you killed."

A soft rumble emanated from Kellen, but one withering look from his alpha quieted him down.

Skyler was scared. Hands shaking, palms sweating, pulse pounding through her like a war drum.

Tagan led them around the back of the trailer. It was dark away from the bonfire, but Drew disappeared, and moments later, strings of holiday lights illuminated an oversize and dilapidated metal roof that protected gym equipment and work-out machines from Mother Nature. Tagan's gaze roved over the dumbbells and a row machine. He took his time choosing, and the more he thought, the more nervous Skyler became. This was so much worse than Denison putting her on the spot and making her sing. This was a job interview. Her freedom could be made or broken here tonight.

Brooke stood behind her mate but watched Skyler with her lips pursed in a thin line.

"I think we'll keep it simple." Tagan pointed to Bruiser, the biggest of the bear shifters. He was taller than a Sasquatch with arms swollen with muscle. "Plank position."

Bruiser dropped down on his hands and tiptoes

without question and waited for the next command.

"You ever done a pushup before?" Tagan asked.

Skyler's stomach clenched, and she nodded miserably. If she'd had any question about whether Tagan wanted her in his crew before now, it would've been squashed with this impossible task he was setting her to. Bruiser looked unbeatable. "I used to instruct skydivers. I had to be physically fit to work my job."

Tagan lifted his chin and looked down at her. "Good. Plank position."

She dropped down and gritted her teeth, focusing on the corner of the metal cage that housed a squat rack.

"You'll go against Bruiser here, pushup for pushup, and if you fall first, you leave tomorrow like you planned."

The snarl was back in Kellen's throat, and he took a stumbling step forward, as if he couldn't help himself. His eyes reflected oddly in the dim light, and he smelled like fur.

"Kellen," Skyler warned as he took a second step toward Tagan.

"If you outlast him," Tagan continued, ignoring

his Second, "then you can come to work tomorrow. After a week, I'll decide whether you are fit for my crew or not. But first, you have to beat old Bruiser over there. Do you still think you want to do this?"

"Yes," she rushed. "I'm going to do this." She sounded much more confident than she felt, thank the stars.

Tagan crossed his arms over his chest, his triceps flexing. If it was for intimidation, it worked. She wished he would get on with it already because her arms and shoulders were already starting to burn. And old Bruiser looked as comfortable as could be.

"Drew," Tagan said, then nodded his chin toward Bruiser.

Slowly, Drew settled onto Bruiser's back.

Relief flooded Skyler, dumping adrenaline into her veins. The task was still utterly impossible, but at least she felt better with Bruiser's added weight. The yeti's arms began to shake, and she gave him a slow, challenging smile.

"Begin," Tagan said in a bored voice.

Skyler lowered herself down.

"One," the Ashe crew counted as she and Bruiser straightened their arms.

"Two."

"Three."

"Four."

Kellen crouched in front of her with a curious smile on his face. "Good," he said. "You can do this."

And suddenly, she felt like she could. Or at least she could give this all she had and be proud of her effort. Tagan was trying to push her off and weed her out, but she didn't have to make it easy for him.

The crew counted, "Five."

"Six."

Tagan was crouching now. "All the way down. Good girl. Bruiser, you too."

"Seven."

"Eight."

A slow smile was creeping over Tagan's face, one that matched Kellen's. If she didn't know any better, she would've called it pride that she saw there.

"Come on, Skyler," Brooke said as she hit fifteen.

When she and Bruiser hit twenty, the rest of the crew began chanting her name, softly at first, then louder with clapping. Brooke dropped down beside her and began to do pushups, too. Skyler's adrenaline surged again with the urge to please Brooke. Arms shaking, muscles burning, Skyler gritted her teeth and struggled to push herself up. She was slowing now, unable to keep up with Bruiser. He watched her carefully and slowed, too.

"Brighton," Tagan said.

Brighton sat next to Drew on Bruiser's back, and the giant man grunted. A drop of sweat dripped down his nose as they hit thirty.

"Don't give up now, Beautiful. You're damned inspiring to watch," Kellen said, eyes intense as he watched her push up on trembling arms.

Her body was on fire. Abs working, body tight, shoulders straining. She couldn't do this.

"You can," Kellen murmured, as if he could see the defeat on her face and read her quitter thoughts.

Bruiser was struggling, and Tagan gestured Denison onto his back, bless that man.

"Fucking do this," Brooke said, lowering herself down beside Skyler for another rep. "Prove him wrong."

"Tagan?" she rasped.

"No," Brooke said, panting. "Prove Roger wrong."

Roger. That was enough to get her blood boiling. He didn't believe she was capable of anything. When she sang, he told her to "cut that shit out." When she cooked, he called it disgusting. He had thrown a full plate at her once! He'd never said a single nice thing to her since the day she met him.

Skyler didn't know why Tagan was testing her limits, but as she grunted and pushed herself up again, she knew it was for a reason. And not some domineering test to embarrass her in front of everyone. He was challenging her to be better than she thought she could be.

Bruiser's arms strained and twitched, and he cursed as he lowered himself again. Except this time he pitched forward and landed with his hands on either side of his massive chest.

Panting, she lifted her steady gaze to Kellen's proud face, then to Tagan's, and with the last bit of strength she had left in her body, she pushed herself up one last time and fell over.

The crew erupted into cheers, and Brooke massaged Skyler's cramping arms, then pulled her upward. She settled her in front of Tagan.

The alpha's eyes sparked with something she couldn't understand. "Be ready by six in the morning," he said. "Probation starts now."

As she watched him walk away, she wanted to please him. Not because she needed his blessing to stay here, but for Kellen, who'd been in trouble with his alpha since she'd arrived. She wanted life to be easier for him, and if she could win his alpha's approval, Kellen could be happier.

Kellen wrapped her up in a hug. "You did so good," he whispered against her ear before passing her to Denison for a ridiculously rough hug.

Bruiser patted her on the back hard enough to rattle her ribs, and Drew squeezed her shoulder so hard that she winced, but she felt good and happy receiving their congratulations. These stranger bears were proud of her for winning a simple pushup contest that was obviously swayed in her favor. They seemed to care if she was inducted into the crew. Seemed to care that she was here. All her life, she'd been treated like an object, but here, amongst these cussing, spitting, beer-guzzling, dominant as hell, shirt-stripping, muscle-bound titans, she was welcome.

As she looked at Kellen, watching her from the outskirts of the circle, she suddenly wanted things.

Wanted a life and friends…and Kellen.

She wanted this feeling to last more than a day or a week.

She wanted to take care of these people who had unknowingly given her one of the most influential and important nights of her life.

She wanted to be part of the Ashe crew.

EIGHT

Skyler stretched her legs out, searching for cool pockets under the soft covers of her bed. It had to be three in the morning, at least, and sleep still eluded her. Between the push-up contest and all of this change she could feel happening inside of her, she should've been exhausted. But instead, she couldn't hold her arms and legs still for more than a minute before she went to fidgeting again.

She had to cut ties with Roger.

It wasn't enough to disappear forever and never have closure. She needed to face him and tell him she was leaving. Tell him he'd messed up when he mistreated her. If she didn't, it would always feel like her heart was half-healed, splayed open, waiting for the last few stitches.

She sat up and pressed the pads of her feet onto the cool floor beside the bed. The room was dark with the blackout curtains covering the windows, but her night vision was excellent. Hooray for shifter senses.

She padded across the room to her oversize purse that sat on top of the dresser. With her phone pulled from the side pocket, she turned it on and waited impatiently. It took forever to turn onto the home screen, or so it seemed as the seconds she spent thinking about what she was going to say to Roger left her hands sweating at the palms.

When the main screen finally glowed through the darkness, it told her she'd missed forty-two calls from Roger. Or as her phone secretly identified him— *Assface.*

That tiny rebellion had made it easier to shoulder the things he said and did. At least when he called, and the uncharitable name she'd given him flashed across the screen, it felt like a tiny victory in a war she'd long ago lost.

There wasn't enough reception for her to call out, so she made her way to the living room and stood on the couch. She shoved the phone upward until it touched the sagging ceiling, but it still didn't have enough bars. Crap.

More determined than ever, she ran into the bedroom and slipped on the jeans she'd borrowed from Brooke, then snuggled into Kellen's jacket he'd lent her. It swallowed her and hung down to her knees, but it smelled of him and made her feel stronger. Strong enough to do this now. Tonight.

The porch didn't offer enough reception, so she made her way to a creaking gate in the fence behind 1010 and onto a worn trail that led up the mountain. The moon was only half full, but that was plenty of light for a shifter like her. Farther and farther she hiked until she reached a ledge that overlooked a valley. She gasped and stared out over the vast wilderness. Stars painted the sky, like glitter on a canvas. Pulling her jacket more soundly around her, she lifted her cell to her face. Three bars. Good enough.

Squaring her shoulders, she punched the call button and settled the speaker against her ear.

Roger asked, "Where are you?"

"I have something to say, and I'd appreciate it if you'd just let me get it out."

"Fuck what you have to say. I've looked everywhere for you. You were supposed to be home when I got back, cooking me a fucking chicken dinner. An edible one this time!"

"Stop yelling at me." Damn that pathetic tremble in her voice.

"I'm not going to ask you again, Skyler. Where. Are. You?"

"I've left you." She held her breath and closed her eyes.

A beat of stunned silence sat heavy between them, and she imagined him running his hands through his greasy blond hair.

"You stupid bitch. Do you even know what you are saying right now?"

"I don't choose you. I want the right to find someone else. Someone who doesn't hate me."

"I don't hate you," he ground out.

"Do you love me?"

"Yes." Lie. It was gross how easily he could do it.

"Then why did you push me the other day? Why

did you laugh when I hit the counter? Why did you leave me there on the floor crying? Why did you call me names as you walked out the door? Do you even know what love is?"

"Love," he repeated, disgust dripping from the word. "You speak of love too much. It's not important to anyone but saps and humans. You have one job to do, Skyler, and you can't even fucking do it. Keep me happy. And when you manage that, bear me offspring and continue my lineage."

"Do you even like kids?" Her voice had wrenched up an octave, but she didn't care. She was in Asheland Mobile Park, long out of his treacherous reach. She was safe.

"What does that have to do with anything? God, you really are as stupid as the council told me you were. Underachiever in finishing school, pain in the ass to your handlers, but did I listen? No. I let your tight ass and fucking delicious-smelling cunt sway me into a bad decision."

Each word he uttered was a blow. Her knees buckled. Heavily, she sat in the dirt and looked helplessly at the starry sky. "Great," she said in a small voice. "Crisis averted. We can both go our separate ways. You can go find a mate who has a shot at pleasing you, poor woman, and I can make my own way without you."

He laughed, a long, cruel sound that bubbled from his chest and bounced around her head. "You're so stupid," he said, still chuckling. "You don't make this decision. I do. I don't want to separate and pick someone else. You want to know why?" His voice dipped low and harsh, all humor gone. "Because your misery makes me happy. You can't hide your disdain for me from your face, and it soothes something in me I can't fix when I'm not winning a war for your precious daddy. And when you come home, Skyler, I'm going to fuck you. No more waiting for the ceremony. No more putting me off. I own you, and I'm going to hurt you, Skyler. That'll be your punishment for thinking you could leave a Crestfall."

"I'd rather be banished than come back to you." There it was, that steel she knew could bolster her voice. The tremble had left her, and in its place was determination. She wasn't his plaything or a spoil of war or revenge on her father for whatever the wars had leached from Roger's humanity. She wasn't just a wet hole for him to force himself into either. She'd rather die than be used by him.

"Do you know what they'll do to you if you are banished? The Welkin Raiders will find you as soon as someone leaks that you've been banished. They won't just kill you, Skyler, you poor, naïve little idiot. They'll break those fragile little bones in your fingers first, then move up. They'll cut away at you until you beg for death, then they'll let you heal and start over. For months. Come home, and I won't tell the council what you've done. Do it now before I lose my patience."

"I can't." She was terrified, shaking so hard she had to hold the phone with both hands. If their enemies caught her, she'd be tortured. But she couldn't go back to the way she was before. She'd been uncaged—had tasted freedom. How could she go back now to that dark place she'd lived in? "I won't."

"You'd rather spend the rest of your short life alone?"

She was going to get that job and stay here with people who cared if she lived or died. With people who saw her as more than some genetic jackpot. With Kellen. "I'm not alone," she whispered, barely strong enough to find her voice. "Not anymore."

****

"You've surprised me," Tagan said from behind.

Kellen jumped and jerked the brake lever, grinding the cables traveling down the mountainside to a halt. He couldn't remember the last time someone had snuck up on him, and it made him more irritable that he already was. "How so?" he gritted out.

"Your mate is down there working with the crew, and you're all the way up here. And you haven't once asked me to switch you out so you could be closer to her." Tagan gripped the cage of the giant machine Kellen operated. "Now, I've known you a long time, and you can't help your protective instincts, but with Skyler, I've watched you avoid her since dawn. What gives?"

"She's not my mate. I'm not made for a—"

"Horseshit."

Kellen growled and searched the hillside below him. When he was sure it was still clear, he hit the lever that dragged a trio of giant logs up the side of the mountain. "What do you want, Tagan? You bled me yesterday, were a pain in the ass last night, and now you're bored of working so you want to piss me off all day? Is that it?"

"Why are you avoiding her Kellen?"

Kellen hit the brake and twisted in his seat. "Why did Brooke leave you?"

Tagan's face morphed into an expression of pain, and his gaze automatically glided over to the hill that Brooke had sat on the day he'd been forced to Turn her. "If you're bringing that up just to hurt me—"

"I'm not. I want to know why."

A distressed muscle twitched just under Tagan's left eye, but Kellen glared him down, waiting.

"She left because she didn't want me coddling her while she tried to get stronger." Tagan angled his head and gave Kellen a dead-eyed look. "That's why you're keeping your distance from Skyler. You don't want her running from you."

"All I want to do is follow her around and do everything for her. I don't want her to have to lift a finger. I want to feed her and bathe her. I want her living in my den, not 1010, so I can hold her if she ever gets scared. I want to pick her up and carry her everywhere, for chrissakes. And last night, I wanted to win this job for her. She did it on her own, though.

If I allow myself to do the things I want for her, eventually, she'll leave. I followed her out into the woods last night. I couldn't help myself. I knew she needed to call Roger on her own, but I trailed her, anyway." He shook his head, disgusted with himself. "And I listened to him call her names over that damned phone line, and I heard the vile way he talked to her, and she didn't even react, Tagan. She's used to it. And all the while she's just taking it, my animal wants to reach through that phone and pull his larynx through his neck. She's already stronger than when I picked her up. Hell, maybe she's stronger than me. But I saw what Brooke went through and the aftermath of her leaving you. I know what I can and can't do, and apparently, my dopey ass can't handle losing Skyler like that. I have to give her space to get stronger on her own so that maybe someday, she'll give me a real shot. And not just because I was the first nice guy to come along and give her positive attention, but because she wants me back."

"I thought you didn't want a mate."

"I don't!" Kellen's headache blazed to life again, rattling his skull. He ran his hands through his hair, massaging his scalp as he steadied his breathing. "I can't have a mate, but it doesn't stop me from wanting Skyler. I'm all mixed up."

Tagan gripped his shoulder and shook him gently. "Welcome to the club, man."

After Tagan leapt from the metal stairs to the ground, Kellen raked his gaze down the hillside to where Denison was teaching Skyler a more efficient way of tying the logs to the cables. She was good. Nimble as she bounded over the piles of felled trees under Denison's direction. It was obvious even from here that she learned fast and was eager to keep her crewmates safe. She'd be good at this if Tagan gave her a shot.

It gutted him. Kellen hadn't been afraid in a long time, but having Skyler under the heavy cables he operated had him carrying some major tension in his shoulders. Rolling his neck, he gritted his teeth and fought the urge to go down there and give Denison the machine. He'd been gunning for a spot up on machinery for a month, and Kellen could protect her better from right beside her, down with the rest of the crew.

But that's not what she needed out here.

She wasn't in danger from her people on the job

site. Not with the crew around. If he went down there and gave into his craving to take care of her every need, she'd stay stunted and unsure of herself. And dammit, she was going to be a tough-as-nails hellion when she built up her confidence. He couldn't wait to see that spitfire spirit he had caught a glimpse of turn into an inferno. She was a volcano, dormant now, but someday, she'd put on one hell of a show.

He had to be patient. He had to give her space to trust herself and her own decision-making abilities.

Right now, he needed to staunch his protective instincts and find a balance between treating her how she deserved and stifling her growth.

NINE

It was pouring buckets of rain, but that wasn't the reason Tagan was calling the shift off early. The slopes were slippery and treacherous and the working conditions miserable. Mudslides were almost constant, and slick logs kept slipping from wet cables. Mud caked on everyone's boots, making it nearly impossible to move without epic concentration. In the past hour, Tagan had barely taken his eyes off the sky. He'd just stood on the edge of the landing, hands on his hips, eyes narrowed, watching the storm roll in. The alpha finally blasted a whistle from above them where the big machinery sat abandoned by Brighton and Kellen.

"Lightning scares Tagan," Denison explained. "If it stays far enough away, he'll keep us working, but this storm is going to barrel down right on top of us."

The roiling storm had blocked all sunlight, making it look much later and darker. And for the last half an hour, the sky had lit up with streaks of electricity blasting from the heavens. A long curl of thunder rumbled so loud it rattled the earth beneath her feet. Skyler stepped over a pair of felled logs, then jumped to the ground behind Denison.

Bruiser jogged past her. As sure-footed as a billy goat, he clapped her on the back and bolted ahead. "You did good today, rookie."

Skyler grimaced. "Hey, how long do I have to work here to get rid of that nickname?"

"More than the week and a half you've been here," Bruiser called over his shoulder.

"So," she said, hopping another pile of logs to catch up with Denison, "why is Tagan afraid of lightning?"

"He and Kellen and his momma, Meredith, used to live in this little house on the outskirts of Saratoga. It was struck by lightning three times and started burning with them sleeping inside of it."

She jerked her gaze up toward the landing. Thank God they'd all made it out. The thought of Kellen burning in his bed was a scene her overactive imagination would likely latch onto for nightmare time when she went to sleep tonight. "Three times? How did they know?"

"An investigator for their insurance company came out because the gas lines were faulty and had gone up like a blowtorch inside the walls. Apparently, they can GPS lightning strikes, and their house was definitely hit three separate times, at least thirty seconds apart. The local news station came out and did a story on them and everything. Their insurance company won a lot of money by suing the company who made the gas lines. It wasn't the first house that had burned because of the faulty lines, and some of the other victims weren't as lucky as Tagan, Kellen, and Meredith. Anyway, the whole lightning never strikes the same place twice belief is bullshit. It's rare, but it happens, and Tagan doesn't like us out here exposed and under all this metal equipment and cables during a storm like this. He's a good alpha. A good leader."

"Is Kellen scared of lightning, too?" she asked, taking Denison's offered hand as he helped her up a muddy embankment.

"Nah. Tagan's not afraid of much. Kellen's afraid of less. He went through way worse when he was a cub. Lightning and burning houses were puppies and kitties compared to what he saw—" Denison drew up short and ran his oversize hand over his face, then flung water from his fingertips. "Shit." Denison turned and shook his head at her. "It's like a talent you have, drawing people into a conversation like that. You have an instinct for when someone isn't paying attention to what they're saying. No more spilling secrets. If Kellen wants you to know anything about what makes him tick, he's going to have to be the one who enlightens you." Water dripped in a constant stream from his hard hat, and another lightning strike nearby lit up his face. Denison narrowed his dove-colored eyes. "I wouldn't mind bargaining, though. A secret for a secret. What kind of shifter are you?"

This was the most fun game of all. She'd been driving Denison and the boys nuts, and it was the only defense she had against their constant ribbing.

She didn't mind the half-hearted insults and nicknames she'd been accumulating from the Ashe crew, but she could sure as hell drive them bat-guano crazy by keeping her animal side to herself. She was pretty sure Kellen and Tagan knew exactly what she was, but they didn't seem inclined to spill the beans either, and sometimes they smiled when she avoided answering, as if they enjoyed the game. And she lived and breathed for that grin on Kellen's face. "Wouldn't you like to know?" She climbed past him, giggling as Denison cursed under his breath.

"Look, we have a bet going on. Whoever gets you to Change takes the pot. The winner will make a few hundred bucks. I'll go halfsies with you if you tell me."

"Denny, Denny, Denny." She clicked her tongue behind her teeth and held onto a slick tree root as she looked back over her shoulder at him. "You cheating little cheatery cheater."

"Damn straight. It's my turn to buy the beer for the crew this week. I need that money."

"Sorry 'bout your bad luck," she called, climbing higher.

"Dammit, Skyler. It's beer for you, too, you know."

"I like the boxed wine Kellen gives me."

So Kellen had survived a house fire, one that according to Denison didn't even scathe him, and he'd gone through rough times when he was a cub. She lived for tidbits of information on Kellen's past like this. He shared almost nothing, clamming up every time she mentioned anything to do with her younger years to try and draw him out. In fact, he clammed up around her about almost anything lately. The man was utterly confusing. He stared at her in a constant fashion, but when she tried to connect, he shut down. The past week and a half had been the best and most revealing time of her life. It had also been the most confusing, thanks to Kellen's apparent regret over their little naked party last week. She tried not to let it hurt her. He'd told her he didn't want a mate from the beginning, but inside, she'd been growing fonder of him by the day. Now, she tiptoed the edge of an affection that was downright terrifying because it seemed the man she'd chosen didn't choose her back.

As if her thoughts had conjured him, Kellen appeared through the rain, leaning against the side of a giant crane-like machine called a processor that stripped entire logs in seconds.

"Payday," Tagan said from right beside her. He handed her an envelope. "You're now a wage-earning tax-payer. Good job, rookie. You earned this."

She stared at the envelope, utterly shocked. She hadn't thought about pay. As strange as that sounded, she really had seen the job as a way to earn her place in 1010 and with her friends.

"Keep it dry, will you?" Tagan said with a grin, then jogged after his crew toward the parked trucks in the make-shift dirt lot across the road from the landing.

"Right," she murmured, tucking the paycheck into the inner pocket of her weatherproof jacket.

When she looked up, Kellen was still standing there in the rain, watching her with intense eyes. His lips were set in a thin line, but when a smile of joy spread across her face, a similar one crooked his lips, too. Her heart stuttered, and her legs felt like she was floating.

With long, excited strides, she approached him, but stopped short. Her instinct was always to hug him after a long day, and she always had to catch herself. This time was different, though. This time, it was Kellen who reached for her. He pulled her in close until the rasp of his sexy facial scruff rubbed against her rain-soaked cheek.

"I'm proud of you," he murmured in a soft stroke against her ear.

Her knees buckled, and she buried her face into the thick folds of his jacket. Those words did something amazing to her—every time. And he used them often, as if he wanted to make sure she knew her efforts were enough.

"I've missed you." The words escaped her throat before she could stop them.

"How could you miss me? I've been right here." Confusion edged his tone.

Unable to explain how she'd missed his touch without sounding pathetic, she shook her head, her cheeks making zipping sounds against his jacket.

"Tell me. I don't understand," he said, easing her back. His eyes sparked with worry as he searched her face.

He was beautiful, drenched to the bone, eyes dark and caring, rain streaking down the sexy whiskers on his face. His nose flared, as if he was testing her scent, but all she could smell was wet earth, moss, and ozone.

"You're sad," he said, voice cracking. "Tell me why. Please."

Why was she sad? She had no reason to be. She'd found a place as an honorary Ashe crew member. She'd found a job, and no one called her names or hurt her anymore. She felt safe for the first time in as long as she could remember, and the best man she'd ever met was looking down at her, gripping her arms like he cared what was wrong with her heart.

But...he'd been pushing her away. He was just a friend, and she wanted more.

Staring at him, strong-framed, long-legged, holding her arms like he wouldn't let her go until she made him understand what was wrong, she couldn't help herself. Standing on her tiptoes and sliding her palms up his chest, she pressed her lips against his.

Kellen froze, and his mouth went rigid for a moment before they softened on hers. She thought he would allow her to kiss him—just a chaste pressure on his lips—but his arms wrapped around her so tight, she couldn't breathe. He lifted her feet off the ground. With a groan of pure pleasure purring up his throat, he plunged his tongue past her lips.

Wrapping her arms around his neck, she gave

into him, her Kellen. Her strong, confusing, sweet-as-pie and protective-as-a-warrior bear.

"I missed you touching me," she whispered as he hoisted her up and pulled her legs around his waist.

His eyes rolled back in his head, and he sighed, as if her words had eased something tight and unmanageable within him.

Her weight seemed to be nothing to him, though his arms were hard and bulged under the fabric of his jacket as he carried her toward his truck. He strode through the mud, his boots making squishy sounds with each step.

The other trucks were gone, the rest of the Ashe crew having headed back down the mountain, and Kellen's jacked-up ride was the only one that remained.

She pressed kisses all over his face and neck until he laughed. "What are you doing, Beautiful?"

"Making up for lost time. You've been distant this week."

"I have reasons for being so."

"Like what?"

When the smile dipped from his face, she cupped his cheeks and kissed him again, softer this time.

"You are a very tricky bear to get to know," she said, bestowing another playful kiss on the tip of his nose. "At least tell me what you are thinking now."

"Want to get you out of these clothes."

"Oh?" She waggled her eyebrows.

"Dirty-minded woman. I mean I want to get you dry." He seemed enraptured with the smile on her face, and he settled her onto the side of the bed of his truck where she was eyelevel with him. "You've changed a lot since I first met you."

Raking her fingernails lightly across the back of his head, just under his hard hat, she asked, "How so?"

"You seem happier. You laugh a lot and make jokes." He traced her lips with the tip of his finger. "You smile."

"I'd smile more if you'd quit pushing me away."

"I don't want to do that. I just want to make sure you're okay before I…"

He was right there, right on the verge of letting her in. "Before you what?"

He looked away at the dark wall of clouds rolling in from the east. "I want to take you into town."

Her heart slammed to the bottom of her feet, and

she froze. He was getting rid of her? Taking her back to Roger? Not now. Not after everything she'd found here. "But I don't want to go back," she rasped through her closing throat.

His dark eyebrows drew down. Rain spattered his yellow hard hat in a storm song as he stared at her. "I'd never take you back to him, Skyler. I meant I want to take you to dinner." His words became rushed. "I've been watching Tagan and Brooke, and she seems to like to go into town for dinner alone with him. I asked her about it, and she said it was good to date. Her voice turned different, like a song, when she talked about spending time with Tagan, and I want that for you."

Skyler's head spun with relief. Feeling dizzy, she leaned her hat against his and sighed her stress out on a breath. "What do you want for you?"

"What do you mean?"

"You said you want that sing-songy feeling for me, but what do you want?"

"You."

His answer drew her up short. Cupping the back of his neck, she closed her eyes and lost herself in the feeling of being wanted by him. She'd thought he didn't see her as a potential partner. He'd slept with her, sure, but she was still learning her way around bear shifters, and they very well could place sex over feelings and emotions. Intimacy was important to her, though, and when she'd shared that part of herself, she'd expected him to open up. When he hadn't, she'd felt lost. And now it seemed like her feet had been slammed back to earth. The journey was dizzying, but so worth it if, at the end of the day, she could feel like this.

"I thought you didn't want me," she admitted, the thick words clogging her throat.

A soft growl rumbled from his chest. The door latch clicked as he yanked it open, then he set her inside the dry cab of his truck and shut the door beside him. She was settled in his lap, nestled against his chest as his breath came unevenly. Without a word, he reached over into the glove compartment and pulled out a tiny, navy-colored box. Slowly, he set it on the passenger's seat, then looked out the window beside him with a slight frown. "I asked Tagan about your people."

Her chest heaved as she stared at the unassuming gift sitting on the seat beside them. With trembling fingers, she lifted it to her lap, then opened it slowly.

Tears stung her eyes as she pulled out the delicate gold chain with the songbird charm. It was no bigger than her pinky nail. Her people exchanged trinkets at a ceremony that bound them as mates. If she accepted this gift, and if she gave him one in return, he would be hers, and she his.

"Do you know how big this is? Or is this just a gift because you want to take me on a date?"

"I bought it the day after you sang with Denison and you won your spot on the crew. I've kept it all this time because I don't want this life for you. I want a better mate for you, one who won't hurt you. One you won't grow to resent. I was trying to figure out how to make you happiest—to let you go or draw you closer." He drew his sad gaze to hers and lowered his voice. "But then you said you missed me touching you, and I can't go back anymore. You're mine."

Skyler cupped the necklace in her palm. "Kellen, I don't want to make you sad." Her heart felt like it was overflowing and breaking all at once. "Why don't you think you would make a good mate?"

"If I tell you, you'll run away from me."

"I won't. You have to trust that I care about you enough to listen and try to understand where you come from."

He stared out the window for a long time, then turned on the truck and scooted her into the passenger's seat.

Geez, why couldn't he just talk to her? He shut down like this every time, leaking out the smallest amount of information possible, which only served to drive her insane with the twenty new questions that arose. And pushing him for more didn't help. If he didn't want to talk about something, he just slammed down a wall she was helpless to break through. She wanted him, all of him, but perhaps Kellen wasn't capable of sharing himself wholly with someone else. Maybe that was the problem. Maybe he knew he was unable to let people in, and he didn't want to hurt her with it. That was the only thing that made sense from the bits and pieces she'd scrapped together from him and Denison.

She placed the necklace back in the box and put it back in the glove compartment, confused as to why he'd given it to her if he had no intention of actually allowing her into his life. And not just the life he had now. Kellen was different. He spoke different, acted different, seemed governed by different rules. Even Tagan made allowances for him that the others in his crew weren't afforded.

Kellen drove her back to the trailer park in silence, his eyes hard on the muddy road in front of them.

She felt duped. Her heart had fallen for someone incapable of returning the depth of her feeling. And sadly, she'd still accept him if he was serious with the necklace. Pathetic.

With her hard hat in hand, she shook out her damp hair and prepared for him to drop her off in front of 1010. Instead, he pulled his truck to a stop in front of 1015, his trailer. She hadn't ever been allowed in there, and from what she'd seen over the past week and a half, no one else ventured in there either. While the shifters in this crew openly walked into each other's trailers—sometimes without knocking as she'd learned when Brighton barged in on her in the shower and snatched a bottle of low dose pain killers from the medicine cabinet before he waved and let himself out—no one ever did that with Kellen's home. He seemed to be very private about his living space, a fact that only made her more curious about her elusive bear.

The crew were out and about, battening down the hatches. They were stacking the plastic furniture around the fire pit, then dragging them to Bruiser's trailer.

She thought Kellen meant to help them, but he cut the engine, jogged around the front of the truck, and opened Skyler's door. With a frustrated sounding grunt and a muttered, "Aw, fuck it," he scooped her up, ran through the torrential downpour, and climbed his porch stairs.

His shoulders heaved in an explosive sigh as he settled her on her feet, just outside the front door.

"Swear you'll try and understand?" he asked.

"Of course," she said in the easiest promise she'd ever made.

He opened the door and pulled her in by the hand. It was unnaturally dark, and she had difficulty shimmying out of her sopping wet jacket. He didn't seem to have the same problem by the sound of fabric rustling against her senses. She waited for him to flip on the light switch, and when he didn't, she asked, "Can we turn on a light?" Her night vision was impeccable, but there was so little illumination to work with, it was hard to see even the couches that were situated just a few feet in front of her.

"Skyler, there aren't any lights. I took them all out when I moved in here. If I need light during the day, I open one of the windows I've boarded up."

She didn't understand. "So, you live in the dark? Like a bat?"

"No, I live in the dark like a bear. This isn't a trailer to me. It's my den. My bear requires it, or I won't have any control."

"Control over your animal?"

"Yes."

His hand was still strong and warm, all wrapped around hers, and she squeezed. "Who else has seen your den?"

"Tagan. He knows how I have to live from when he and his mom took me in."

"Tagan…and me?" It was heartbreaking that he had to live in the dark because of his inner animal, but he was sharing something huge with her. Something that scared him and made him hide from other people. He was letting her in.

"The others probably know, but it's something I

don't share. My bear, he doesn't like others in his territory."

"But he's okay with me in here?"

"My bear chose you before I even knew you. You'll always be safe in here with him. With me."

"Will you show me around?"

"Sure. Wait here." His hand disappeared and, moments later, a thin stream of gray light appeared from behind a piece of plywood Kellen scooted off a window. The living room and kitchen were the mirror opposite of 1010 with the kitchen on the right-hand side. A gray couch and love seat sat in front of a mahogany stand with a flat screen television. The coffee table and end tables matched, and a painting of the processor Brighton operated hung on the wall. It was done in thick, dark paints with neon green and blue highlights, and in the background, the sky was littered with stars. A hurried but skilled brush had created the landscape, but the processor was detailed down to the last screw.

"Brooke paints," Kellen murmured.

Skyler had only ever seen the pictures of Brooke's attacker. She sometimes studied them when she was alone in 1010 and organized them into piles.

They were mesmerizing, but this? This was incredible. Brooke had captured the mountain and the job site in a way Skyler never would've thought possible. She stepped around the couch and looked at it closer. "It's stunning."

She moved onto the kitchen with its whitewashed cabinets and quaint wooden cutouts. A countertop separated it from the living room. The sink was empty, and clean dishes were stacked on a drying rack. A small, two-seat table sat against the wall with a stack of outdoor magazines as the centerpiece. His furnishings weren't what she'd expected. They were sparse and minimal but of fine quality. Everything seemed to be in its place, as if his bear couldn't tolerate clutter.

Kellen watched her with an unfathomable expression as she moved around his space. His dark eyes never left her as she smiled and moved to his bedroom. Like the rest of the den, it was neat and orderly. His bed was made, the navy comforter wrinkle free, as if it was ready for a catalogue picture. A cup of water sat on the nightstand, and she brushed her finger down the cool glass before she turned.

Steeling herself, she squinted at his dark

silhouette across the room and asked, "Kellen, why do you have to live in the dark?"

Kellen hesitated, lingering at the door. The dark stole his facial expressions, so she couldn't tell if he was shutting down on her again or not. After a pregnant pause, he approached slowly and lay on his bed.

"Come here."

"My clothes are wet. Will your bear get angry if I mess up your bed?" She didn't understand the dynamics, nor had she realized how much his animal ruled his life. Her animal side wasn't like that—a separate personality. Her inner animal was just an extension of herself.

"I don't care about the bed. I want it to smell like you, anyway. Maybe then I can sleep better."

She lowered herself to the mattress and laid her head on his chest. "Would you sleep better if I slept beside you?"

His heart went to pounding like a bass drum against her ear, and she smiled. Hide his feelings all he wanted, but he couldn't put a poker face on his heartbeat.

"Yes. I didn't think you would want to sleep in a

place like this. You are light and happy, and this place is dark."

"This place is a part of you, and I want to be with you. Besides, I don't need light when I sleep."

Voice deep and sure, he said, "Then yes. And I live in a den because growing up, I didn't feel safe."

"Your dad?" She'd pieced together that his father had been bad news.

Kellen sniffed. "My dad wanted his cub to be the toughest bear that ever was. He thought letting me sleep in beds would make me soft and weak, so he raised me like the animal inside of me—like a bear. I slept in the woods—no tent, no mattress, separated from my family, no matter if it rained or snowed—until the old bastard died when I was ten."

"Oh, my gosh," she said on a sad sigh. "Where was your mother?"

"He was beating on her. She didn't have any say in how I was raised. Eventually, she left."

Skyler clutched his shirt and squeezed her eyes closed against the image of Kellen sleeping all alone, cold and afraid out in the woods, every single night. "Were you angry when she left?"

"Yeah. I didn't blame her for leaving, though. I

was mad she didn't take me with her. She was living out on a mountainside in a broken down bus they'd converted to a home. Who could blame her for moving on from that? My uncle would come visit every few months, bring us food and try to talk my dad out of his paranoia. Dad thought humans would find us out, so I didn't see or talk to anyone outside of my family until he died and I wandered into the nearest town. I didn't know how to talk to anyone. Still don't. It makes me...feel different, like an outsider. People don't understand me, and I don't understand them."

Everything made sense now. Every single thing she'd been confused about clicked quietly into place. His hatred for men who hurt women, his need to lift her up and make her strong. The way he talked and how he discussed shifter matters within earshot of humans. How he watched others as if he was studying them, how he kept his past hidden. No wonder he'd locked these secrets away. She would've done the same thing to protect herself.

"Were you happy when you went to live with Tagan? Were you able to be a child?"

Kellen huffed a humorless laugh. "Poor Meredith

didn't know what to do with me for the first two years. I was much worse off than I am now, I can tell you that. But yeah, I was happy. I am happy, but some of the stuff I went through is just part of me now. I won't be rehabilitated. I'm just…me."

"Kellen?" she asked, hugging his waist and snuggling against his side. "How do bears claim a mate?"

He froze under her touch, every muscle rigid. "The males bite the females during sex, hard enough to leave a scar. We mark our mates. I wouldn't be any good at being a mate, though. We would have to be something different. Something less."

"Disagree. I think you would make a wonderful mate. Who told you that? Who said you would be bad at it?"

"My mother." His voice dipped to a ragged-sounding whisper. "She would cry and say I looked just like my father. That I'd grow up to be just like him, a monster."

Skyler hunched in on herself at the pain in those words. What a terrible set of parents he'd had. What a terrible life they'd provided for him. Even if his mom was hurt by her mate, she shouldn't have taken it out on her child.

"Kellen, I want you." Her voice trembled, and she dashed her hand across her damp lashes. "I want you because I know the truth. I know you would be a wonderful mate. You are nothing like your father, do you understand? You brought me here to save me. You've lifted me up at every opportunity. I'm stronger because of you. You gave me the necklace because you pick me, right?"

In the dark, she could barely see him, but she could feel him nod his head, hear the whisper of his hair against the comforter.

"Well, I pick you back. Fuck what your mother said. I know you. I *see* you. Your heart is too big to ever hurt me. I love the life you've given me, and I love the way you treat me. I love your den. I love…I love you, Kellen. Everything about you. None of this scares me off. It only makes me feel closer to you."

Kellen's breath hitched, and he pressed his forefinger and thumb against his eyes.

She pulled him up and straddled him, tugged his shirt over his head, then tossed it to the floor. When her own shirt and bra joined the pile, she hugged him up tight until there was no end to her and no beginning to him. Her chilled skin warmed against his, and when his shoulders stopped shaking, she eased back and cupped his cheeks.

"You're mine, Kellen Cade Brown. I don't care what anyone else says. Our relationship is different because we're different, and that's okay with me."

He rested his forehead against hers. "I want you, too. I'll mark you when you're ready."

A slow smile of sheer joy stretched her face. Her heart was wide open and raw from the emotions of the last two weeks, but she wasn't exhausted from the upheaval like she should've been. Instead, she felt alive for the first time in forever, and Kellen was a huge part of why she could smile again. She thought she hadn't had a choice when Roger picked her, but she'd been lied to.

The choice in a mate was hers.

The choice in a mate was Kellen's.

Kellen kissed her slow and easy, brushing his fingertips lightly up and down her back, conjuring gooseflesh as she bowed against him.

Skyler brushed her lips down his jawline, then his neck, and rested her chin on his shoulder. With a private grin at how lucky she'd been after all, she closed her eyes and whispered, "I'm ready now."

TEN

"Where do you want my mark?" Kellen asked on a breath.

"Someplace where everyone can see it."

"I don't want to hurt you." His hips swayed against her thighs, pressing the thick roll of his erection against her jeans.

"I'll be honored to bear your mark."

He nodded and cupped her breast in his warm palm. "It is my honor that you've chosen me to be your mate, Beautiful."

Her heart fluttered at the nickname. Out of all the ones the Ashe crew called her, this one was her favorite. Kellen had gifted it to her when she'd felt worthless and hideous. It was the first word that began this incredible transformation inside of her.

Kellen undressed her the rest of the way, then shucked his pants and pulled back the comforter. When she was tucked up, dry and warm beside him under the covers, he rolled her onto her side and pulled her back against his chest. A delicious tremble shook up her spine at the feel of his taut chest against the tender skin across her shoulder blades.

"What was that?" Humor laced his question.

Heat blazed up Skyler's cheeks, and she was thankful he wouldn't be able to see it in the dark. She closed her eyes and focused on the way his finger trailed fire up her side. "I like the way you touch me," she whispered, afraid to break the spell he cast on her.

His cock, hard as stone, pressed against her lower back as he tucked his hips forward. Gooseflesh sprang up under his fingers When he dragged his fingers softly over the curve of her shoulder, gooseflesh sprang up under his touch.

"Good," he murmured.

His tongue touched the back of her neck just

before his soft lips did. He gripped her hip as he allowed his teeth to scrape her skin. Was this it? Would he mark her now, or was this just a tease? She arched her back and exposed her neck, pressing against his erection. His hold on her hip tightened, and a quiet growl of approval rumbled up his throat.

She could feel the vibration against her spine and gasped as he touched his teeth to her neck again. Wetness pooled between her legs.

Reaching back, she ran her fingertips through his hair and pulled him closer to her, exposing her throat even more, encouraging him.

He chuckled deep in his throat. "You do want my mark, don't you, little songbird?"

A whimper escaped her lips as she nodded. She wanted it more than she'd ever wanted anything. With his claiming mark on her skin, she'd belong to him, a man worthy of her affection.

He nudged his knee between her legs and lifted upward until she was spread wide. Her body curled backward against him as he pumped his erection slowly against her spine. With a strong grip, he pressed his thumbs into her lower back, then angled her hips toward him.

"I was told your people mate from behind," he whispered against her ear, just before plucking her sensitive lobe between his lips. "Would you like that?"

She was panting now, desperate for him to touch the wetness he'd conjured between her legs. "Please," she begged. "Yes."

Kellen eased his hips away, and when he pressed against her backside again, his long cock slid against her crease, the head of it touching her clit just barely before he pulled back. Oh, that tease. She was going to explode if he didn't fill her.

"Kellen?" she whimpered.

He ran his hand across the swell of her hip then up her ribcage, slowly drawing another tremble from her body. He was so close, his cock sliding against her wetness, teasing her entrance.

He grazed his teeth against her neck again, and she arched deeply against him. The sharp canines disappeared, only to be replaced by his soft lips as he sucked on her skin. He reached around to the front of her and cupped her sex. She bucked helplessly against his palm.

"I'm going to come," she panted out in warning.

She felt his lips stretch in a smile against her neck. He pulled his hand away, and she reached back and gripped his hair in an effort to stop the throbbing that was building inside of her. All of her nerve endings were on fire, and any touch from him now would be dangerous. She was riled up and just on the edge as he pressed his cock through her wet heat again. Just shy of her sensitive spot, he pulled back.

Kellen let out a long breath as he gripped her waist and slid into her. Her body stretched around him, and she let out a groan at the feel of him moving within her.

Slipping his hand between the sheets and her side, he wrapped her up in a tight embrace and squeezed her breast. Tweaking her nipple gently, he pulled out of her slowly, torturously, then thrust into her again.

"Faster," she begged.

Kellen's fingers dug into her waist at her request, and he jerked forward, as if he were losing control. As he pulled out of her much too slowly again, his muscles shook.

"Please, Kellen. Faster!"

His stomach contracted forward again, forcing

him to fill her. This time he rolled his hips slightly faster, and she closed her eyes. This, right here, this was what making love should be like. It wasn't supposed to be used for pain, like Roger had threatened. It wasn't supposed to degrade her or make her feel dirty. Sex wasn't a weapon. This, what Kellen was doing to her now, was bonding her to him in a way she never could've imagined. Each tender caress made her love him even more. Made her devotion to him run deeper.

Kellen didn't know how to fuck her. He only knew how to worship her body.

Louder and louder, her voice lifted in a groan of ecstasy every time he pressed into her, until he began bucking hard. His careful control was slipping away, and the growl in his throat became more feral with every sound of pleasure she made.

He flipped her on her hands and knees and slammed into her from behind, rocking her forward then back. His body pressed against the length of her spine, and his lips found her neck on the next thrust. His teeth touched her skin, her nerve endings firing just at her hair line.

Each powerful thrust, she was sure he'd pierce

her skin and claim her. Pressure spread through her abdomen until she couldn't contain it anymore.

He was waiting for something. He'd been careful with her, caring. He'd said once that he wanted the choice to be hers.

"Kellen," she gasped. "I choose you."

He cupped her sex and slammed into her just as his teeth penetrated the skin at the back of her neck. Pain and pleasure clashed, blinding her until she cried out. Her body tensed around him as he swelled within her, and as he forced his elongating teeth down into her muscle so his mark would scar and remain forever, another wave of orgasm consumed her.

He thrust into her in such a fast rhythm, all she could do was lock her elbows and hope her arms held as pulsing waves of pleasure crashed through her like an ocean surge against the sand. Kellen froze, biting down as he groaned. His seed poured into her, warming her from the inside out. He pushed forward again as a second jet shot into her, then a third.

Caught between pain and bliss, she cried out as his bite released her. Skyler's arms trembled so badly, she fell forward onto her elbows. Why was she crying?

Kellen's tongue stroked where warmth streamed down her throat. Over and over, he lapped at her, cleaning her, soothing her. "It's done," he murmured in her ear.

Kisses trailed around the injury, and when his weight disappeared from her, she thought he would pull out and cradle her. Instead, he kept his connection, deep within her, and ran his strong hands up and down her back, massaging, petting, and relaxing her.

Locking one arm against the mattress beside her, he reached under her and kneaded her breasts, then he cleaned the wound again. It felt better already. Part of it was her shifter healing, repairing the muscles that had been ripped open, but it was more than that.

Kellen was healing her—heart, soul, and body— with his careful attentions.

His cock grew hard within her again, but he didn't seek pleasure for himself. Instead, he pulled out, rolled her over gently, propped a pillow under her neck, and kissed her lips. She could taste iron on his tongue from where he'd cleaned her, but it only made her love him more. He hadn't wanted to hurt her, but he'd been strong. Done what was necessary to claim her, then taken care with her afterward.

Her gentle bear—her tender mate.

He lowered himself and sucked on her sensitive nipples in turn, then trailed his lips down her stomach. Her breath froze as his mouth brushed her clit. With such tenderness, he kissed and sucked and lapped until she came again. With her hands in his hair, guiding him, she didn't scream out like she had earlier. This time, his name came on a breath of gratitude as he brought her to climax slowly. And when her aftershocks ceased, he climbed up beside her and tucked her neatly against his chest where she was safe and warm.

"My mother was wrong," he whispered in the dark. "I won't be like my father. I'll work hard to make you happy every day. I promise to be the mate you deserve."

A tear slipped out of the corner of her eye and landed with a tiny splat against the pillow. Running her hand down the smooth planes of his back, she burrowed in closer to him. "You already are."

ELEVEN

A tremendous banging noise jolted Skyler awake. Her body flung backward so fast, her stomach dipped to her toes before she was still again. She seemed to be pressed between the headboard and the wide expanse of Kellen's back. She couldn't see a damned thing in Kellen's den.

"Rain stopped," Bruiser called through the thin wall. "We need your truck."

The tight knots in Kellen's shoulder muscles relaxed. "Idiots," he muttered, stumbling from the bed.

"What's happening?" Skyler asked, heart still

lodged somewhere between her throat and her brain. "Is someone hurt?"

"No," Kellen said in an inhuman snarl. The rustle of fabric sounded from somewhere to her left, and she squinted at the darker figure. He seemed to be struggling into a pair of jeans. "The boys like to go night muddin' when the weather is like this."

"Right. Night muddin'. Are you going with them?"

"You want to come, too?"

It was the middle of the night, and by all accounts, she should be exhausted after the emotional roller coaster of yesterday, but Bruiser banging on the echoing trailer walls had frightened her wide awake. "I want to be with you."

The mattress sank in around her and Kellen's lips landed on hers, as if he could see her just fine in the darkness of his den. "Good."

"I need to get some fresh clothes and get ready, though. It'll take me five minutes."

He gripped her ass as he pulled her up, then nibbled on her neck. She bathed in his attention, smiling into the darkness as he worked his lips downward to the base of her throat.

"Kellen, hurry up!" Drew yelled through the wall.

Kellen's growl was nothing shy of feral. With a sigh, he helped her dress in her discarded clothes that he seemed to find just fine in the pitch black, then led her to the front door.

With a triumphant swat on her ass, he winked and said, "I'll see you in five...mate."

A giggle peeled from her throat as heat crept into her cheeks. *Mate.* Just that word from his lips sent riotous flutters into her middle.

He gripped the railing of his porch as she walked across the street. Twice she looked back at him, and both times he watched her with hunger and pride evident in his gaze.

The trailer park was lit by strands of holiday lights that zigzagged this way and that between and around the trailers. There weren't any streetlights, but the tiny firefly-looking lights made up for it with quantity. The Ashe crew was busy piling out of their trailers and loading into trucks.

"Holy shit, rookie," Denison said as he sauntered toward Tagan's trailer. "What happened to your neck?" He shoved a strand of her hair to the side and made a hissing sound behind his teeth.

Well, now that he mentioned it, Kellen's mark

hurt like a mother trucker, throbbing and burning like it had been waiting for someone to notice to spring up and pain-attack her.

"It looks like someone..." Denison's eyes went wide. "Bit you," he finished quietly.

His narrowed eyes lifted to hers, and she couldn't help the big, dumb grin that cracked open her face.

"Are you shitting me?" he asked. "Kellen! Is she shitting me?"

Kellen cocked his head to the side and gave Denison a proud smile. "She's mine," he confirmed.

"Two in one night. Two in one night! Brooke!" Denison was running around in circles now, as if he didn't know what to do with himself.

"What are you squawking about, man?" Bruiser asked, sliding from behind the wheel of Denison's old, beat-up Bronco.

Brighton, Haydan, and Drew jogged over, followed by Tagan and Brooke.

"What's happened?" Brooke asked.

So happy she thought she'd burst from it, Skyler lifted up her hair and showed them Kellen's mark. "I'm claimed." Tears stung her eyes as the Ashe crew surged forward.

Suddenly, Kellen was there, shaking under the claps on his back and rough hugs, and she was swept up in Brighton's arms, feet completely off the ground. Brooke pulled her down just as Tagan wrapped Kellen in a hug and slapped him on the back. The alpha said something too low for her to hear in Kellen's ear, and her mate answered with an emotional smile.

Tears streaked Brooke's face as she shook Skyler's shoulders gently. "We're Ashe crew now."

Skyler frowned, uncertain what Brooke meant. "What?"

Brooke turned and pulled her shirt down over her shoulder. On the muscle just above her shoulder blade was a claiming mark as dark and angry-looking as her own felt.

"Brooke," she breathed. "Tagan claimed you?"

Brooke's face crumpled, and a soft sob left her throat as she nodded. Skyler wrapped her arms around her friend's neck and rocked slowly from side to side, burying her face against Brooke's uninjured shoulder.

Voice thick, Brooke said, "I always wanted a

sister, and now it feels like I have one."

God, this feeling inside of Skyler...it was almost too much happiness. She looked down at her arm, surprised she wasn't aglow with it. Rough arms wrapped around her and Brooke, then another set, and another, until the entirety of the Ashe crew was squeezing the breath out of her.

Skyler laughed breathlessly. "No more all boys club."

"Thank God," Denison crowed. "Too many dicks made it super boring around here."

"All right, all right," Tagan said, voice growly. "The girls are both hurt and need time to heal before you ruffians squish the life out of them like this. Let 'em loose."

The anaconda death grip loosened, and she grinned at Brooke as she wiped her damp cheeks with the back of her hand. "Congratulations."

Brooke's delicate nostrils flared, and it looked like the second round of waterworks were on their way. "You, too. You got yourself a good man now, Skyler Drake."

"Okay, enough with the mushy shit. We doing this or what?" Bruiser called over his shoulder. He was already jogging back toward the Bronco.

Tagan tossed Brighton a set of keys and said, "You and Denny take my truck. Brooke and I will ride with them." He jerked his head toward Skyler and Kellen.

"Why?" Denison asked.

"Because Kellen is the best mudder out of all of us, and you're a front seat driver. We'll lead."

Kellen scooped Skyler up and carried her toward his white monster truck. He looked relieved and so satisfied he was practically seeping happiness. She cupped his cheeks, his short scruff rough against her hands. She lived to see him like this. He wasn't confused or overthinking everything like he'd been doing. He was just open. Free.

"Oh!" Skyler exclaimed, remembering. "I was supposed to change clothes."

Kellen leaned down until his nose touched her throat. "These clothes are fine. You smell like me."

Which was great and all, but she was about to share a small space with Tagan and Brooke.

"I haven't changed my clothes yet either," Brooke said low.

Well, all right then. Nobody here seemed to care

about this stuff, so why should Skyler stress herself out over it?

Kellen settled her behind the wheel, then she scooted over to make room for him. Tagan lifted Brooke onto his lap, and his mate rested her palms against the roof of the cab as if she knew rough roads were coming.

Skyler had never been mudding before, and a sense of overwhelming excitement took her. Utterly beside herself, she clenched her hands and squealed.

"Excited?" Kellen asked, eyes glued to her smile.

"Yes!" This was the best day of her life. How could she not be excited? Her future with Kellen stretched on and on now. There was no more questioning her place beside him, and after that giant sexyman-woodcutter-werebear group hug back there, she was feeling like this was exactly the place she'd always meant to end up, among the Ashe crew with the man who could protect her heart.

Tagan nuzzled Brooke's neck, and she giggled as Kellen turned the key. The engine roared to life, and he rested his hand on Skyler's thigh as he twisted in his seat and backed the giant truck out of its parking spot.

He took the main road out of the trailer park, the one he'd brought her in on when he'd kidnapped her. She laughed at the memory of how scared she'd been of Roger's reaction when he found her gone. It was a relief how gloriously little she'd thought about him this past week and a half. Who cared about her name and bloodline? No one here. And someday, she'd bear Kellen little cubs and raise them with a man she knew would be an amazing father. But for now, she was happy just being with him. Of making his den her home and making him as happy as he made her. If this truck had a sunroof, she'd thrust herself out into the open air and spread her arms wide to catch the air.

She couldn't wipe the grin off her face as Kellen jerked the truck into the woods and over the first skid of mud. The truck whipped this way and that as he maneuvered a hole-riddled road these trailer park bears had probably used many times before. The truck bounced and spun out, splashing rooster tails of the brown goop whenever Kellen made a sharp turn. The other two trucks and Bronco raced beside them, then rushed ahead as the back of Kellen's ride got bogged down in a marshy area. Headlights flashed this way and that over the piney woods as the bear shifters skidded circles over a meadow.

Drew was hanging out of one of the trucks, yelling in pure joy, hands out above his head as Haydan grinned from the driver's side. Skyler hadn't stopped laughing since they left, and even when Kellen's truck got hopelessly stuck and Tagan convinced her and Brooke to get out and help push them out, she still had a muddy grin on after they were done with the messy work.

A quick glance in the rearview showed her happy reflection, mud streaked across her face where she'd scratched an itch. Kellen hooked his arm around her shoulders and brought her in close, then kissed her like he meant it. His lips spoke the words he'd told her earlier. He loved her. Adored her, just like she did him.

And when they finally drove home and said goodnight to the crew, he tugged her hand and led her to 1010. In the light of the bathroom, he peeled her filthy clothes off her. The bathtub was ancient, a baby-puke brown color, and definitely lacked the stopper to run a bath, but Kellen plugged up the drain with a shaving cream cap, filled it with hot water, and bathed her slowly from her hair to her toes.

He didn't say anything as he worked, but he didn't have to. His gaze cherished her body and warmed her from her belly to her fingertips. When her skin shone like an eggshell in sunlight, he checked the mark he'd made on the back of her neck, turned off the lights, and fell asleep beside her, tucked up tight and warm under the comforter.

And that was a gift in itself. Tonight, Kellen had given up his den for her.

As she watched him sleep beside her, breathing deeply, his heavy arm slung over her waist, she marveled at how much her life had changed—at how much he'd changed it.

She brushed her fingers over his cheek and inhaled his scent.

He would protect her as long as she lived.

And as long as he lived, she would do the same for him.

TWELVE

"Do you miss my giant flannel shirt?" Skyler teased.

Kellen laughed and shook his head, then opened his mouth for another bite of frozen yogurt Skyler offered him from her cup.

He swallowed and draped his arm across her shoulders. "I prefer you in this outfit." He raked his gaze down her tank top and borrowed dark-wash skinny jeans tucked into her black hiking boots. And finally, he took in the gold songbird necklace she proudly wore around her throat.

"Now, if you were comfortable wearing that

flannel potato sack," he continued, "you know I'd still love you in it, but you dress more confidently now. I like you strong."

"It's all my new lumberjack muscles. I have to show them off." She flexed her arm, and he arched his eyebrows appropriately.

He hadn't stopped smiling on their entire date to the Snowy Mountain Pub and to the ice cream shop after lunch. Kellen had laughed more today than she'd ever seen him do, and it lightened her step with every booming sound of amusement he gifted her with.

Saratoga was busy for a Tuesday afternoon, but she didn't mind the crowded sidewalk. Nothing could bust up her mood. She was newly mated to a man she hadn't dreamed of wishing for. He acted honored that she was with him, touching her constantly in affectionate ways.

"I like your hair up like this," he said, cupping the casual messy bun she'd pulled back and away from her face with a hair band. "I can see your eyes better."

"You like it because it shows off my mark," she accused happily.

"That, too." He leaned down and kissed her

earlobe. "I think you like showin' it off."

"Hell yeah, I do."

"What about this one," he said, pulling her to a stop in front of another clothing boutique.

His hand was already full of shopping bags, but he seemed determined she get whatever she wanted. Her new paycheck was already half-spent on new clothes and personal items she needed for her new home, but she'd lived simply for so long that more than a couple weeks' worth of outfits seemed frivolous.

"Nah, I think I'm good. Do you need to get anything while we're in town? I think you've paid your dues shopping with me today. I owe you."

"I like shopping with you," he said, confusion drawing his eyebrows into a frown. "I like when you show me your clothes and want to know what I think. No one has ever cared about my opinion like that before."

"I want to look pretty for you," she admitted, lacing her fingers with his and bumping his shoulder. "It makes me feel good when you look at me like you are right now. Like I'm the prettiest thing you've ever seen."

"You are."

She shrugged her shoulders up near her ears with giddiness and sighed at the butterflies he conjured in her belly.

He kissed her knuckles and steered her toward the grocery store. "Tagan gave me a list of stuff he and the boys need from town. That was the deal. If he synced up our days off, I had to take care of groceries again this week for the crew. We have a big number to hit by Saturday."

"Yeah, I heard the log buyer is coming, and the big boss has almost doubled the lumber order."

"Are your muscles still sore?" Kellen asked, massaging her neck gently.

She glanced across the street before they crossed at the light and skidded to a stop. Roger stood there, staring at her with vitriol in his cold eyes. A truck pulling a trailer stacked five rows deep with stripped logs drove between them, and when it passed, Roger was nowhere to be seen.

"Skyler?" Kellen asked, worry thickening his tone. "What's wrong?"

"I...I thought I saw..." She swallowed hard and tried to steady her galloping heartbeat.

Kellen searched the other side of the street and pulled her closer. "Hey," he said low. "Even if he's here, you're safe. Skyler." He hooked a finger under her chin and drew her attention upward to his eyes. "He won't hurt you. I won't let him." Kellen's eyes churned an odd color. Silver gray in the saturated sunlight.

Shaking her head to rid herself of the chills that had taken her, she touched where Kellen's smile lines had disappeared. "I know. I was just startled is all. I'm not even sure he was really there or if I imagined him."

Slowly, Kellen leaned down and brushed his lips against hers. She relaxed instantly, her muscles losing their tension as she clutched his black, cotton T-shirt. Damn, but her man looked good today. His V-neck shirt stretched tight over his defined chest, and his jeans hung just right on that sexy waist of his. His boots were big and clunky, just the way she liked them, and his hair was perfectly mussed, begging her to run her fingernails across his scalp. And those silvery inhuman eyes? Her knees were knocking by the time he brushed his tongue against hers.

His fingers gripped her hair as he angled her face

and deepened the kiss. His other hand found the curve of her backside.

"Get a room," a passerby muttered.

Skyler giggled and eased back, but Kellen only cocked his head in confusion at the irritated man.

"What does that mean?"

"It means he doesn't appreciate our PDA."

"What's PDA?"

"Public display of affection. 'Get a room' is a saying that means we should do what we're doing in a bedroom, in private, not out in the open where people can see us."

"Oh. But I like kissing you."

She couldn't help her grin any more than she could help the rain. "I like you kissing me, too. It's probably the ass grabbing that has him grumpy."

"Oh." Kellen removed his kneading hand from her derriere, then picked up the bags he'd dropped. "Fine. Later we'll get a room. In our den."

"It's a date."

"It is? I thought we just went on a date. Brooke specifically said a date is when you go into town and go out to eat or watch a movie."

Skyler giggled and tugged his hand as the walk

sign on the pedestrian light flashed. They crossed the street and meandered into the grocery store to start in on the giant list Kellen had tucked in his pocket.

As they passed the floral section, Kellen asked, "What is your favorite flower?"

"Pink roses." She said it without thinking. Her favorite used to be tulips, but now, she adored the rose she'd pressed dry in the center of a phone book in 1010, the flower Kellen had given her the day he decided to take her home with him.

Kellen picked out a bouquet of pink roses and another of yellow. Skyler didn't mind that he picked out flowers for Brooke, too. It was just his way. He cared about women and liked for them to feel special. His kind heart made her adore him even more.

When they had the groceries piled high in the cart and were standing in line at the checkout counter, Kellen patted her butt and muttered, "I forgot Brooke's bacon. I'll be right back. Don't pay," he said over his shoulder, "I got this."

He'd been trying to pay for everything all day. It was clear he liked to take care of her. His bear had a distinct need to feel like a protector and provider, but she'd won by arguing her need to be independent, which he agreed was good for her. She didn't think he'd let her get away with sneaky-paying for the crew's groceries, though, so she began to load everything on the conveyer belt more slowly than necessary.

"You look different." That deep, emotionless voice shot fear straight into her gut. Roger leaned against the stand of plastic bags, arms crossed and head cocked, as if he'd been there the entire time, watching her. His blond hair looked unkempt, as always, and the blue in his eyes was particularly icy.

Skyler squared her shoulders and glared. "I'm happy now. Happiness changes a lot about a person."

"I can see that." His empty eyes dragged to her tight jeans then back to her face. He didn't look amused that she'd worn clothes he would've thrown into the street. "You haven't been picking up your phone."

"I turned it off. I don't have any interest in talking to you. I said what I had to say. We're finished."

The cashier was a heavyset woman with gray, frizzy hair and a disapproving grimace. She looked decidedly uncomfortable with what was transpiring.

"Excuse us," Roger said to the woman.

He wrenched Skyler's arm so fast she squeaked in surprised pain. With an unbreakable grip, he dragged her outside.

"The fuck you say to me? We're over? That's not your call to make."

Fear clogged her throat, but she had to be strong now. She wasn't just some breeder with a pretty name anymore. She was part of the Ashe crew, chosen mate to a strong and good man. She was a lumberjack, a wage earner. She was a laugher, a joker, a lover, a friend. She was so much more than the nothing he'd tried to turn her into. Gritting her teeth to bolster her confidence, she pulled his credit cards from her wallet and tried to hand them to him with a prim tilt to her chin. "Take these back. I don't need them. I guess I never really did."

A cruel smile stretched his thin lips, and he wrapped his hand around her throat and pushed her backward into a thin alleyway. Her boots dragged the asphalt as she struggled against his grip, but Roger was too strong. He slammed her against the brick wall of the store as she scrabbled with desperate fingers to loosen his steely grasp on her neck.

When she struggled to draw breath, choking sounds wrenched from deep within her.

"I thought I made myself clear on the phone that this isn't through. You're still mine."

"Think again, dickface," Kellen said casually from his position leaning against the wall. "Do your dumb ass a favor before you embarrass yourself further and check her neck. Go on, I'll wait. Though, if you don't remove your hands from my mate's throat, I'm going to rip your intestines out through your trachea."

The hard steel in Kellen's voice said he wasn't bluffing. Maybe he really would do that. Skyler wouldn't put it past his bear.

Roger glared at her mate, but his grip loosened. Probably a smart move since Kellen had six inches on him and a fucking *grizzly bear* living inside of him.

She helped the idiot out and turned her head so he could see Kellen's claiming mark.

"What does that mean?" Fury infused Roger's words. "What the fuck have you done?"

"I got myself claimed by a real man." She had to force the words past her aching windpipe, but her voice had stopped shaking, so there was that. "He even gave me a gold necklace."

Roger's eyes turned livid as they landed on her songbird charm. Crimson crept up his neck. "You stupid bitch! You were supposed to be mine! I chose you. I won you. Your father promised you to me." He lifted his open palm and drew it back.

Kellen was there in a blur. One second, he was leaning against the building, and the next he was gripping Roger's hand, stopping him from the open palm slap across her face he'd intended.

"My alpha forbade me to kill you, you sorry sonofabitch, and that is the only reason you are drawing a breath right now. Listen to me. Let this sink in. You'll let her go because you have no choice. I would fucking *eat you* before I let you near her again. You hurt a woman, which means you are not a man. How did you ever expect to keep a woman like Skyler if you can't even treat her with respect?" Kellen's grip tightened on his extended arm, and Roger yelped in pain. "You are a worthless sack of shit, not worthy of breathing the same air as *my mate*. Approach either of us again, and you'll regret that decision."

He let go of Roger's wrist and shoved him so hard Roger's back smashed into the brick wall of the next building.

Skyler rubbed her neck and tossed his credit cards to the ground. "See you when I see you, Roger." Without a backward glance, she followed her future from the dusty alleyway and left her past behind.

THIRTEEN

"Werewombat," Denison guessed.

"Nope," Skyler muttered as she hopped onto another log.

"Werechicken," he guessed again.

"Nope," she answered.

Haydan pulled on a loop of cable to test the strength before he hooked it to a log and propped his leg up on a felled tree. "What if the reason she hasn't changed is because she can't breathe air like the rest of us?"

Denison scrunched up his face and looked at him like he was a dumbass. "What the hell does that even mean?"

Haydan lifted his dark eyebrows and guessed, "Weregoldfish."

Denison perked up and stared expectantly at Skyler.

"Nope," she muttered again.

Kellen shook his head and snatched another loop of cable from Haydan. The boys had been dicking around all morning trying to figure his mate out, and so far hadn't managed to even get close. Skyler scaled the log he was eyeing and stood on the other side, then helped guide the cable around and handed it back to Kellen.

She was good. Really good. Efficient at her job, hardworking, caught on fast, never complained, and was the first one out there and loaded up in the truck every morning. Her capability still hadn't stopped his bear from revolting every time he sat up in the machinery above and toted thousands of pounds of lumber much too close to his mate. He'd put in a request to Tagan a week ago to work with the rest of the crew doing the manual labor down on the hillside. Now his alpha ran the cables that dragged the lumber up to the landing, and Brighton was still running the processor after Connor had been killed. And when they needed a bobcat to drag the clean logs to the truck to haul them into town, well, Drew had stepped up, leaving Denison, Bruiser, Haydan, himself, and Skyler to work the mountainside, unless someone had a day off. Today, everyone was at the job site, even Brooke, who was drawing on a sketchpad from the safest place Tagan could find above the landing.

Kellen's bear had settled with the new routine, and if he was honest, he enjoyed the physical part of this job. He'd forgotten how strenuous and consuming it was. And damn did he sleep well at night now. Though he couldn't tell if that was from the hard work, scaling the hillside and lifting all day, or from fulfilling his mate's needs in their bedroom.

The thought of her joining him in the shower this morning, and him slipping into her under the hot jets of water was enough to bring a contented rumble to his throat.

As Denison went down a list of were-farm-animals, Kellen had to bite his cheek to stop from cuffing his friend upside the head. It was getting old, and Skyler had stopped smiling about it early this morning. She hadn't Changed since she'd arrived three weeks ago, as far as he knew. Now, he could go a while without turning into his bear if he absolutely needed to, but it was uncomfortable to stay in one form too long. From the way Skyler had been cocking her head this way and that in jerky motions, it was clear just thinking about her animal was wrenching up her level of discomfort.

Why wouldn't she just Change?

It couldn't be the game. Sure, it was funny as hell watching Denison slowly sink into madness trying to figure her out. The rest of the crew, too. They'd been pestering him and Tagan non-stop trying to get them to spill the details of Skyler's animal. But if she was hell-bent on keeping it to herself for now, he and Tagan would respect that.

With the trio of logs looped with cable, the crew made their way toward the tree line, well out of the way of the skyline cable above them. When they were all clear, Kellen pulled a handheld whistle from his pocket and blasted it twice, signaling to his alpha it was safe to bring down the line. Tagan sent down a box with three heavy dangling metal cords to attach to the cable loops on the logs.

Another whistle blew in the distance, and Kellen narrowed his eyes at the sound. The Gray Backs were the other crew in these mountains, and for whatever reason, the head boss who owned this land had placed their current job sites too close. Bear shifter crews were territorial for one, but for two, if they came any closer, Tagan wouldn't be able to tell between his whistle and theirs, and it would be dangerous if those heavy cables came flying down the mountain with them still working on the hillside.

Chop, chop, chop. Kellen scented the air and frowned at the sound that shouldn't have been in their territory. The rest of the Ashe crew went silent, too. The discord echoed over the mountain. It could be on the edge of the jobsite or a mile away. It was hard to tell.

"Is that the Gray Backs?" Bruiser asked, resting his hands on a low-lying pine tree limb above his head.

"Shouldn't be the Boarlanders," Kellen murmured. The crew of cutters had already felled all the trees for both job sites and wouldn't be on this side of the mountain working their chainsaws today. "I think you're right. It must be the Gray Backs."

Skyler was looking up at the sky in silence, unblinking.

Kellen touched her cheek. "Come back to earth, Beautiful. It's okay. Probably just the Gray Backs taking down a missed tree or re-running their skyline. It happens."

Skyler made an attempt to smile and dipped her chin. Another jerk of her head as she angled her face, and he was hurting for her. He wished she would just Change. She had her reasons for keeping her animal hidden, though, and she had shut down any conversation he'd started about Turning. He'd Changed into his bear three times this week, and twice she'd come into the woods with him, following silently as he foraged, explored, and fished in the stream, as if she just wanted to be near him whether he was animal or man. He loved her for her unconditional acceptance, but she wasn't giving him anything in return with her animal side.

Maybe she didn't trust him completely yet, or perhaps her people didn't need to Change as much. Or maybe it hurt to let her animal out, and that's why she was putting it off.

Whatever the hold-up was, he wished with

everything he had she would share that part of herself with him. She was open with everything else but that.

The chopping continued, the sound ricocheting off the mountains, but Kellen lifted his mate's hand and kissed the knuckles of her work gloves. "Come on," he ordered the crew. "The cables are ready, and we have a deadline to keep."

In a rush, they stepped, jumped, and ran over the piles of fallen logs. Most of the trees here were dead from the beetle infestation, which is why the man who owned this land had hired the two crews to clear it. They were replanting as they went, hoping for new forest to spring up. As it was now, all of the dry, dead timber was basically a matchbox waiting for someone to throw a cigarette out a car window and light this place to bloody blazes.

Kellen grabbed the first dangling cable that hung from the skyline above them and hooked it to the loop they'd attached to the log earlier. Skyler and Haydan worked on the second log while Denison worked the third. Bruiser was already preparing loops for the next set of logs to haul when the chopping became louder and the skyline lurched dangerously.

Tagan yelled something Kellen couldn't understand from the landing above, and when he looked up, his alpha and Brighton were running toward the tree the skyline was attached to.

The towering tree was falling, taking the line with it, and it had nowhere to go but down the mountainside. It would take other trees with it, creating an avalanche of lumber.

"Get out of the way!" he yelled, pointing to the tree line.

"It's a distraction," Skyler murmured.

Time slowed as he watched her terror-filled eyes shift from the falling logs barreling toward them to the sky. Behind her, the men were running for safety, but she hadn't moved.

"Skyler, run!" Kellen yelled, too far away from her.

Horror widened her eyes as her gaze locked on something above him. Her jaw clenched as she bent her knees, bunching her muscles. With an explosion of power, a falcon exploded from her, and she shot straight toward him, wings tucked, with an avian battle cry in her throat.

No, not straight for him. She was aimed just above him. When he turned his face upward, a pair of lethal looking talons were catapulting down on him, straight for his eyes.

A blast of feathers burst from the attacker as Skyler hit him side-on. The giant birds fell to the ground as another screech blasted from her throat.

Roger. The bigger falcon was slashing with his nails and beating his powerful wings, but Skyler was holding her own, and the feathers on his chest were turning red.

The crashing sound of the trees tumbling toward them was deafening, and just as Skyler disengaged, Roger beat his wings and lifted into the air.

Something was wrong. Skyler was flapping furiously but wasn't getting anywhere. Her wings must have been injured. Kellen squinted at her. Beautiful gold and cream feathers, blazing green eyes riveted on her enemy, curved blood-soaked beak that sharpened down to a dagger-like point. Black talons stretched out as if she was waiting for Roger to attack again. She was beautiful. But her wings...they didn't look like Roger's. Her biggest feathers had been damaged somehow, and she was unable to fly.

"Skyler," Kellen yelled, running for her. He had to protect her from the tree-slide if she couldn't escape with flight.

Roger passed him with his wings tucked, and at the last moment, he spread them wide and latched his talons onto Skyler's.

"No!" Kellen pumped his legs over the piled lumber and reached for her, but it was too late.

Roger thrashed his wings above Kellen's reach, dragging Skyler higher and higher toward the dark clouds above.

Her green eyes locked on Kellen's, and she looked so sad, so scared.

"Fuck!" he screamed, gripping his hair.

The first falling tree sailed over him. Kellen ducked out of the way of the second and third. The crew was yelling in the background, but he couldn't understand what they said. He couldn't understand anything. His bear was roaring to get out of him, but he had to hold onto his human side for a while more. He had to survive this slide so he could try and save his mate. His focus was rattled, and he jumped over a falling log, only to be drummed in the head and shoulder by a thinner one. Pain zinged down his body and warmth trickled down his face as he ran toward the tree line at a break in the avalanching lumber.

"What do we do?" Denison asked as soon as he was out of the way.

"She can't fly!" Kellen rasped out, panicked. "Her wings are messed up."

Denison's gaze jerked skyward. "Oh, my God."

"Spread out and catch her," Kellen ordered.

Bruiser was already relaying the message into a walkie-talkie to Tagan up on the landing, but Denison pointed to the sky. "There she is."

Roger and Skyler had just hit the clouds, and although their forms were faint, they were visible.

Kellen took off, his grizzly bursting from him in a blindingly painful moment of fur and teeth and claws cutting through his flesh. He was quick as a man, but he was much faster as an animal.

Behind him, he could hear the panting of his crew as they Changed and followed him. When they reached the middle of the cleared lane, the bears behind him spread out.

Kellen watched the sky. *Please don't let him drop her somewhere else.*

Down to his marrow, Kellen knew he wouldn't.

Roger would drop her where Kellen could watch her die. It was a coward's revenge, and Roger was as spineless as they came.

Kellen huffed a breath as he saw something fall through the clouds. Skyler was flapping her wings uselessly, trying to slow herself down.

Hold on, beautiful.

She was too far ahead, would land at the other end of the jobsite. The distance was too great. Fear pulsed through his blood, dumping adrenaline into him and urging his legs to pump faster. He dug his claws in and pushed his muscles until he was as close to flying as a bear could get.

She was in a free fall, spinning uncontrollably as she tried to catch the wind with her damaged wings. A cry burst from her throat as she approached the tops of the trees.

Almost there. Almost.

As she blasted toward the ground in front of him, he leapt through the air and stretched his paws as far as he could, then tucked around her at the last moment. He skidded across the blanket of pine needles and slammed into the trunk of a towering spruce.

Afraid to look, he stared at the clouds she'd fallen from, panting so hard his chest burned. Slowly, he opened his claws and looked down at the bird of prey that lay across his chest.

Skyler's eyes were closed.

No.

Kellen's breath caught as he sat up and cradled her. Grunts of snarling agony clawed up his throat as he stroked the back of his paw down her chin to the top of her neck, like he'd done the first day he'd met her on that bench outside the grocery store. His fierce little falcon had saved his eyes from Roger's talons. His shifter healing could do wonders, but re-growing body parts was beyond him. Roger had meant to take his sight, and Skyler had attacked him with single-minded fearlessness. His strong mate. His Skyler.

Her eyes fluttered open, and the feathers on her breast fluffed as she struggled to sit up. Whatever had happened to her wings had destroyed her sense of balance. Kellen closed his eyes, and as relief washed over him, he melted back into his human skin. With a heaving sigh, he pressed his arm under her talons and she latched on. Her blade-sharp nails drew tiny streams of crimson from his skin where they pierced him. He didn't care about the pain. She couldn't help that her body was all weapons.

The Ashe crew appeared through the trees, transforming from their bears back into their human skins.

"You're a falcon," Denison said softly.

Skyler's sharp beak was open as she panted, her feathers ruffling with each breath. Kellen didn't know much about birds, or what kind of falcon she was, but she was likely much larger than any found in the wild. She was heavy on his arm and her talons were easily two inches long. His mate could do some serious damage in a fight. Roger had flown away colored in red, but as Kellen searched Skyler's body, he couldn't find a single cut.

Pride swelled in his chest at how fierce his mate was, and he held his arm up higher as Tagan made his way through the trees, Brooke following closely behind.

A slow smile of respect took his alpha's lips, and another wave of relief washed over Kellen. He loved Tagan like a brother, and his approval of his chosen mate meant the world.

As Kellen adjusted her heavy weight, Skyler

spread her wings, as if to try and keep her balance. Kellen narrowed his gaze onto her biggest feathers, which had been clipped neatly in half.

Something red and awful snaked into his gut, conjuring a low snarl. "Did he do this to you? Roger. Did he clip your wings?"

She couldn't answer in this form, but she didn't have to. The sadness that consumed her beautiful green eyes ripped his heart out.

He turned his gaze to Tagan. "Grant me vengeance."

The muscles in Tagan's jaw twitched and jumped as he clenched his teeth and sighed. His hard, blue eyes drifted to Skyler's clipped wings, then back to Kellen. He nodded once, then held out his arm.

Rage boiled Kellen's blood, and he clenched his hand as he passed Skyler off onto his best friend's forearm.

"Denison," Tagan murmured, then jerked his head up toward the landing.

Denison followed silently behind him as Kellen made his way toward his truck. He wouldn't return until he avenged what had been done to his mate. The bastard had clipped her, taken the sky away from her.

No wonder she hadn't wanted to Change. Roger had stolen the most important thing to a flight-shifter, just because he could. *Monster.* Roger had mutilated Skyler, then dropped her from the clouds to die in a dishonorable death for her kind.

Kellen had taken a silent oath the day he claimed her. He'd sworn to himself he would protect her, but she'd already been damaged beyond what he had seen.

Such atrocities couldn't go unpunished.

Crestfall or no, Roger was going to pay for what he'd done in blood.

FOURTEEN

Skyler latched onto Brooke's outstretched arm and flapped her wings slowly to try and keep her balance. Ever since she'd been clipped, her animal didn't work well. She knew everyone had been waiting for her to Change, but the more time that passed, the more self-conscious she'd become. At first, it had been embarrassing to admit what Roger had done. The bruises on her face had been shameful enough, but this? He'd *clipped* her.

Sadness pooled in Brighton's eyes as he handed Brooke Skyler's folded up clothes she'd slipped out of when she'd Changed.

"I'm going to take her up on the landing and see if she can Change back. You boys give us some privacy for a while, okay?"

"You got it," Haydan said, and the others murmured similar sentiments.

Brooke made her way steadily up the mountain, only slipping on the steep embankment once. And when she was at the top of the landing, she strode toward the trucks. Kellen's was gone, but Tagan's sat there, dark and shiny against the greenery behind. If Skyler's weight on her arm or sharp talons bothered Brooke, she didn't complain. Brooke settled her onto the lowered bed of Tagan's truck, then unfolded her clothes and sat down beside her.

"I don't think you can Change back as easily as bear shifters can, and I didn't want you feeling rushed around the boys down there. They will have to set up a new skyline now, and that will probably take them the rest of the day." Brooke nudged her softly, her blond waves twitching with her movement, and she smiled. "Besides, I don't know how you are with nudity around the boys, but I'm definitely not used to it yet."

And that was one of the many reasons Skyler

adored Brooke. She understood things without ever having to discuss them first. She was sweet and sensitive and had an intuition that the rough-and-tumble boys in the crew lacked. Skyler closed her eyes and forced the change back into her human skin. It hurt because she hadn't done it in a while, but she was glad to have the transformation done. It was the first time she'd allowed her animal to have her body since Roger had clipped her.

Her muscles were stiff and sore, but Brooke seemed to know what she needed and helped her dress.

"Is Kellen going to kill Roger?" Skyler asked as quiet as a breath.

Brooke inhaled slowly and nodded. "Yes. What Roger's done to you is too much for a man like Kellen to bear. If he didn't, Tagan would probably go after him, or Denison, or any of the boys down there."

"He deserves death," Tagan said as he approached from the dirt road. "He and whoever was helping him attacked the entire crew to exact a vengeance that was unwarranted. Here." He handed her a cell phone. "Call your council."

Fear trilled down Skyler's spine at the thought of

talking to her father or any of the council again. She'd thought this was through and she'd got a clean break. But Tagan was her alpha now, and he didn't ask meaningless requests. Not like Roger had done. He was a good man, and she trusted him.

She dialed her father's number. He would be in the office with the other council members, but it was the only number she knew from heart.

Dad answered on the second ring. "Hello."

"It's me. Skyler."

"You. You've caused some serious problems for me. You've disgraced our family, your lineage." He sounded disgusted to even talk to her.

"Dad, you disgraced your family when you gave me to Roger Crestfall. I'm not calling to get your approval on my new life. I'm calling as a courtesy and because my new alpha has asked me to do so."

"New alpha?" Dad sounded baffled.

Tagan took the phone from her hand and nodded, as if she'd done well. Relief fluttered in her stomach. Between Kellen and Tagan, she was going to be all right.

"This is Tagan James," he said into the phone. "Do you know who I am?" His eyes went dead and cold. "Good. Then you'll know that I don't bluff, and neither do my people. Skyler Drake is no longer a breeder for your people. She is now Skyler Brown of the Ashe crew. She lives under our protection, works under our protection, and is claimed and mated to the Second in my crew. And I assure you, he is one scary sonofabitch when his mate is threatened."

Tears filled Skyler's eyes, and she lifted her chin proudly as she listened to Tagan initiate her into his crew. She had people now. Real people who cared what happened to her. She'd seen them when she was falling from the sky, running like their lives depended on it, when it was really her life that depended on them—a line of great grizzly bears trying to save her. Why? Not because she was a Drake, but because she mattered to them.

"We have been attacked by one of your own in our territory," Tagan said low, his voice turning gravelly and inhuman. "If this happens again, I will personally take it as a declaration of war between the falcons and bear shifters. Now, I've heard talk that you are already losing a war. Best you don't start another with my people."

He was quiet for a minute as Dad spoke too low

for her to hear on the other end of the line.

"Accepted. Here she is." He handed the phone back to Skyler.

Slowly, she pulled it up to her ear.

"Is this your choice?" Dad asked, sounding defeated.

"Yes. I've chosen my mate and my people. When you chose for me, I got hurt. The only one who knows what is right for me is me."

"You'll forsake your people then? You'll curse your children with bears inside of them?"

"Happily. Because it isn't a curse. When my mate and I decide to breed, our children will be loved by their father and by me, no matter which animal they harbor. My last name didn't ever do anything for me but bring me pain." She wiped her eyes and sniffed, then steadied her voice. "I'm happy now. I've found a place I belong with people who care about me. I hope you can understand."

Dad was quiet for a long time. When at last he spoke, his voice sounded quiet and sad. "Goodbye, Skyler."

"Bye, Dad." As she hung up the phone, she knew it was the last time she'd ever talk to him. Her banishment would be swift, and she'd be shunned by her people. Her father, being a council member, would be punished severely if he ever contacted her, and he wasn't the kind to break his people's narrow-minded rules for sentiment.

She handed the phone to Tagan. He turned and strode off, but right as he was about to disappear over the ledge of the landing, he called over his shoulder, "You're off probation, rookie."

****

It had been hours, and Kellen still wasn't back yet.

Skyler paced 1010 like a caged animal, and when she'd nearly walked off the top layer of cheap wood-laminate flooring, she headed outside to get some fresh air.

The evening was quiet. Most days, the boys cooked or grilled food for everyone around the fire pit at the end of the pothole-riddled street, but tonight, everyone was eating inside. A somber mood had descended onto the trailer park, and if she had to guess, the others were just as worried about how long it was taking Kellen and Denison to return as she was. What if Roger had caught them by surprise and something awful had happened to them. It would be all her fault. She'd brought trouble to the crew, and she'd hate herself forever if anything happened to any one of them because of her.

And if something happened to Kellen? She swallowed the lump of fear down and jogged across the street to Brooke and Tagan's trailer. After her knuckles wrapped softly against the door, Tagan answered.

With a knowing look, he said, "Come on in. You hungry? We have leftovers."

"I don't think I could eat anything right now."

"He'll be fine. I know Kellen. I've known him most of his life. He's one of the best fighters I've ever seen. Denison, too." Tagan squeezed her shoulder, and a curious warmth spread through her chest, relaxing her.

Apparently, Tagan also possessed some alpha magical mojo that could settle her down. With a steadying inhalation of breath, she did her best to smile. It likely came across as a grimace.

"Brooke's in her studio."

"Thanks," she said on a breath, then headed for the second bedroom they'd turned into an artist's haven. Buckets of paints, charcoal, brushes, and inks lined the farthest wall. The floor was covered in a thick, paint-spattered purple rug, and painted canvases leaned against the shortest walls. In the center of the room, a single light illuminated an easel that supported a giant canvas. This was where Brooke sat, dragging a brush down a painting of a falcon.

Skyler gasped at its beauty. Not of her animal, as she was depicted on the canvas, but of the detail Brooke had painted onto it. The paints had been built up, layer upon layer and dark. The lower corner was covered with a drawing of Kellen looking up at the falcon, his arm out as if he were ready for her to land on his forearm. The falcon had its wings spread wide as she prepared to latch onto him with her talons.

Skyler approached slowly. She ran her fingers just above the full-length flight feathers Brooke had painted. The wings were perfect, just as hers used to be.

Brooke hooked her arm around Skyler's waist and rested her head on her hip. "They'll grow back, won't they?"

Emotion clogged her throat, and she nodded. "In

another five months. Maybe less." Five more months, and she'd be able to ride the currents of the wind again and feel the misty clouds on her face. Five more months, and she'd be whole again.

"Can I buy this painting?" she asked reverently as she stroked Brooke's hair. "When you're finished with it, can I buy it for Kellen?"

"No."

Skyler's heart sank.

"I'm painting this for you and Kellen as a claiming gift. I'll take it to Boulder and put it in a show in a couple of months with my other pieces, but I won't list it for sale. When it comes back, it'll be yours."

Skyler smiled and tried to keep the overwhelming urge to cry inside of her. She studied the long cream and gold feathers and the graceful arc of her black talons. "You've made me look quite beautiful."

Brooked squeezed her waist and said, "You are. Someday you'll see that when the damage Roger has done is in your past. When you've had time to heal. This," she said, pointing to the painting, "is what people see."

"Skyler," Tagan called from the other room.

"Yeah?"

"Your mate's back."

Those words had her scrambling out of Tagan's trailer like her tail feathers had been lit on fire. Sure enough, Kellen's truck was pulling to a stop in front of his den. A sob lodged in her throat as she ran toward it.

He slid from the driver's side door as Denison opened the passenger's. She flung herself into Kellen's barely ready arms and buried her face against his chest.

With a growl, he picked her up and kicked his door closed, then took his porch stairs two at a time and hurried them into his den. He'd been leaving the windows only half boarded up lately. He said it was because he didn't like not being able to see her, but she thought it was also from him wanting her to be happy in his home. The darkness had been hard to get used to for her falcon, so his bear was compromising.

He slammed the door and cupped her face. "I don't care," he said, kissing her hard and drawing back. "I don't care that your wings are clipped, do you hear me? You're flawless. My perfect…" He kissed her nose. "Beautiful…" He kissed her cheek. "Mate."

"Oh, Kellen," she sighed as her heart tethered itself to him completely. "I was scared of Changing and you being disappointed. You always look so proud when I do something strong, and I was so ashamed of what Roger had done. Of what I'd allowed him to do to me. I should've fought him harder. Fought until I died to keep my wings. He stripped my pride, and I just cried and took it. I didn't want you to see how weak I'd been."

"You aren't weak. He was."

"Was," she repeated, feeling light-headed.

Kellen stretched out her fingers and laid a long feather across the palm of her hand. It was dark brown with thin white stripes, a marker of the Crestfall lineage. "Was," he repeated. "He won't ever hurt you again. No more looking at the sky, thinking that someday he'll be there. He's gone. It's over."

A mass of emotions flooded her. Sadness at the loss of a life. Heartache that Kellen had been forced to take that life on her behalf. Relief that the fear would finally be over. If Roger had only let her go, he could've survived this. Instead, he had turned murderous and pissed off her mate and an entire crew of fearsome grizzlies. Roger had made his death bed with the first beat of his wings as he dragged her toward the clouds today.

"They'll grow back," she whispered, desperate to show Kellen she wouldn't be broken forever.

"Good," Kellen rumbled as he stroked her cheek with the pad of his thumb. "I'd love you just the same either way, but you deserve the sky. You deserve everything."

She looked around his den, made brighter because he loved her. She held his hands, the ones that had avenged the wrong done to her. She looked in his churning, silver, inhuman eyes, the ones always filled with adoration when he looked at her.

He'd given her a place with his people and a home she felt safe in.

He'd given her peace and encouraged her to find her own inner strength.

She smiled up at him, her protective mate. "You've already given me everything."

EPILOGUE

"I have something for you," Skyler said.

Kellen pulled his sweater over his taut abs and frowned. "You got me a present?"

His dark hair was all mussed from dressing, and she laughed at how adorable he looked, all hopeful and disheveled and undeniably delicious.

He'd ripped all the boards off the windows over time, citing the need to see her body and watch her sleep in the mornings. She'd moved out of 1010 a couple of months ago and into his trailer, which had only seemed to soothe his bear even more.

"Remember when you gave me my songbird

necklace, and I told you mated pairs in my culture exchange gifts in a ceremony to make it official?"

"Yeah?"

"Well, I realized I hadn't given you anything in return. I know we're officially mated according to crew law, but I wanted it to be official in every way."

Kellen picked her up and spun as he fell backward, landing on the mattress with her giggling on top of his chest.

"Give me," he murmured.

She handed him the tiny box wrapped in homemade paper Brooke had taught her to make. "It's not much, but it's the most important thing I own, and I want you to have it."

His face grew serious as he plucked the box from her fingertips. He opened it slowly, as if savoring the moment, then pulled the bauble from the crinkling tissue paper inside.

It was the metal bottle top from the soda he'd given her the first day he'd met her. She had pocketed it and kept it all this time as a reminder of the day her life changed forever for the better. She'd drilled two holes and attached it to an adjustable leather strap.

"I didn't know you kept this," he said, his eyes

riveted on the trinket.

"I've been carrying it my pocket for months. It was my good luck charm."

He inhaled deeply and asked, "Will you put it on me?"

She straddled his hips and opened the leather adjuster wider, then slipped it over his hand and tightened it against his wrist. Dark metal top and dark leather, and it looked very manly, just like her mate.

He cupped the back of her head and brought her down for a kiss. He took his time, softening his lips against hers as he sipped at her, tasting her. His tongue brushed hers, but he seemed content to remain connected in this sweet embrace. She wondered if he even knew he owned her heart and soul.

"Are you ready?" he whispered as he eased back.

Nervous flutters filled her belly again. Was she ready to fly? Half a year on the ground had seemed like an eternity. "Hell yeah, I'm ready."

"That's my girl," he said in that sexy, deep, rumbling voice of his.

She undressed in a rush and gave him a nervous

grin before she let her animal have her skin. Her falcon burst from her, and she settled onto the floor by the bed. She stretched her wings, now completely regrown with long, elegant feathers, and took a couple of practice flaps. The air under her whooshed away, toppling a pair of her shoes that sat against the wall.

"Come on, Beautiful. It's time for you to fly." Kellen offered his arm, and she gripped it with her talons, then spread her wings to balance herself as he lifted her.

She could see everything in this body. The grain in the wooden door as Kellen opened it. And each individual, dried piece of late November grass as he walked her toward the gathering near the bonfire.

The boys were throwing her a First Flight party, but really, they used any excuse to drink beer and barbecue, no matter that it was thirty degrees outside and smelled like snow. They were currently drinking Dixie cup shots of boxed wine with Brooke and laughing at something Denison said. Brighton was strumming his guitar and was the first to see them approach. He kicked his twin brother and Denison turned.

"Aw, yeah, here she comes," Denison called. "You still owe me twenty bucks," he said, glaring at Haydan.

"You didn't get her to Turn!" Hayden argued. "That Crestfall prick did. Technically, he'd get the pot. If he were still alive."

"We had a side bet," Denison said. "Whoever guessed her got the secondary pot."

"You didn't guess her," Bruiser gritted out.

Denison's mouth dropped open as if he was appalled. "I didn't guess her? Are you serious right now? I guessed werebumblebee. I was the closest. I win. Pay up, suckas."

"Good grief," Kellen muttered.

Tagan took a swig of his beer and waved his hand. "Hold on. How the hell do you think a bumblebee is anything like a freaking dagger-clawed, dive-bombing, badass bird of prey falcon?"

Denison arched his eyebrows like the answer should've been obvious. "Bees fly."

The boys erupted into more argument, and Brooke shook her head and took another swig from her Dixie cup. If Skyler could've laughed in this form, she would've. God, she loved being a part of this crazy crew.

"You can do this," Kellen murmured as he crouched down. With a jerk of his arm, she was airborne, stretching long unused muscles as she used the breeze to lift her.

A few more powerful thrusts, and she was high above them, circling her people. They'd all gone quiet as they watched her. Except for Denison. Denison whistled a catcall. Tagan put his arm around his mate, and he and Brooke grinned up at her. Haydan and Brighton lifted their beers in a silent toast, and Kellen...her Kellen. His eyes followed her like she was the most beautiful thing he'd seen. He rubbed the bracelet on his wrist. Her declaration that he was hers for always.

She widened the loop and pumped her wings for higher altitude. Bursting through the clouds, she spun and dove, then pulled up again. Here, she finally felt like herself again. Not her old self that was weak and out of options. She felt like the self she'd always wanted to be.

As she coasted high above the piney mountains, past the clearing where she'd called Roger and told him they were through, and along the mountainside that was home to the Ashe crew's job site, she thought of all she'd found here. When she turned back to get a bird's eye view of Asheford Drive and the trailer park she considered home, she was filled with consuming joy.

The Ashe crew was sitting around the fire, talking, but her mate was still standing just where he'd been, eyes to the sky, waiting for her as he always would.

Kellen had been worth all of the personal growth she'd needed to go through in order to find herself. She'd put in the work and evicted her demons because he deserved the best of her.

She'd risen from the ashes of her past to give herself a shot at happiness with the man she loved.

Today, she didn't feel like a falcon.

She felt like a phoenix.

Want More of the Saw Bears?

The Complete Series is Available Now

Other books in this series:

Lumberjack Werebear
(Saw Bears, Book 1)

Timberman Werebear
(Saw Bears, Book 3)

Sawman Werebear
(Saw Bears, Book 4)

Axman Werebear
(Saw Bears, Book 5)

Woodsman Werebear
(Saw Bears, Book 6)

Lumberman Werebear
(Saw Bears, Book 7)

About the Author

T.S. Joyce is devoted to bringing hot shifter romances to readers. Hungry alpha males are her calling card, and the wilder the men, the more she'll make them pour their hearts out. She werebear swears there'll be no swooning heroines in her books. It takes tough-as-nails women to handle her shifters.

Experienced at handling an alpha male of her own, she lives in a tiny town, outside of a tiny city, and devotes her life to writing big stories. Foodie, wolf whisperer, ninja, thief of tiny bottles of awesome smelling hotel shampoo, nap connoisseur, movie fanatic, and zombie slayer, and most of this bio is true.

Bear Shifters? Check

Smoldering Alpha Hotness? Double Check

Sexy Scenes? Fasten up your girdles, ladies and gents, it's gonna to be a wild ride.

For more information on T. S. Joyce's work,
visit her website at
www.tsjoyce.com

Printed in Great Britain
by Amazon